ms

# RIDGE

# RIDGE

**TEXAS BOUDREAU BROTHERHOOD**

By
KATHY IVAN

# COPYRIGHT

Ridge – Original Copyright © June 2020 by Kathy Ivan

Cover by Elizabeth Mackay

Release date: June 2020
Print Edition

All Rights Reserved

# RIDGE – Texas Boudreau Brotherhood

*Nothing says nice to meet you like a loaded shotgun.*

A notorious drug cartel is using Maggie White's property as a shortcut to transport heroin across Texas. It's up to undercover DEA agent Ridge Boudreau to stop the deadly shipment, and determine if the shotgun-wielding beauty is as innocent as his heart wants to believe or neck deep in a pack of lies.

# BOOKS BY KATHY IVAN

www.kathyivan.com/books.html

## TEXAS BOUDREAU BROTHERHOOD

Rafe

Antonio

Brody

Ridge

Lucas (coming soon)

## NEW ORLEANS CONNECTION SERIES

Desperate Choices

Connor's Gamble

Relentless Pursuit

Ultimate Betrayal

Keeping Secrets

Sex, Lies and Apple Pies

Deadly Justice

Wicked Obsession

Hidden Agenda

Spies Like Us

Fatal Intentions

New Orleans Connection Series Box Set: Books 1-3

New Orleans Connection Series Box Set: Books 4-7

Hello Readers,

Welcome to Shiloh Springs, Texas! Don't you just love a small Texas town, where the people are neighborly, the gossip plentiful, and the heroes are...well, heroic, not to mention easy on the eyes! I love everything about Texas, which I why I've made the great state my home for over thirty years. There's no other place like it. From the delicious Tex-Mex food and downhome barbecue, the majestic scenery, and friendly atmosphere, the people and places of the Lone Star state are as unique and colorful as you'll find anywhere.

The Texas Boudreau Brotherhood series centers around a group of foster brothers, men who would have ended up in the system if not for Douglas and Patricia Boudreau. Instead of being hardened by life and circumstances beyond their control, they found a family who loved and accepted them, and gave them a place to call home. Sometimes brotherhood is more than sharing the same DNA.

This is Ridge Boudreau's story, and Ridge came alive to me the moment I started writing about him. Maggie is the perfect heroine for somebody like Ridge, because she's a feisty, independent woman with secrets of her own, and keeps Ridge constantly on his toes, trying to figure her out.

If you've read my other romantic suspense books (the New Orleans Connection series and Cajun Connection series), you'll be familiar with the Boudreau name. Turns out there are a whole lot of Boudreaus out there, just itching to have their stories told. (Douglas is the brother of Gator Boudreau, patriarch of the New Orleans branch of the

Boudreau family.)

So, sit back and relax. The pace of small-living might be less hectic than the big city, but small towns hold secrets, excitement, and heroes to ride to the rescue. And who doesn't love a Texas cowboy?

Kathy Ivan

# EDITORIAL REVIEWS

"In Shiloh Springs, Kathy Ivan has crafted warm, engaging characters that will steal your heart and a mystery that will keep you reading to the very last page."

—Barb Han, *USA TODAY* and Publisher's Weekly Bestselling Author

"Kathy Ivan's books are addictive, you can't read just one."

—Susan Stoker, NYT Bestselling Author

"Kathy Ivan's books give you everything you're looking for and so much more."

—Geri Foster, USA Today and NYT Bestselling Author of the Falcon Securities Series

"This is the first I have read from Kathy Ivan and it won't be the last."

—Night Owl Reviews

"I highly recommend Desperate Choices. Readers can't go wrong here!"

—Melissa, Joyfully Reviewed

"I loved how the author wove a very intricate storyline with plenty of intriguing details that led to the final reveal…"

—Night Owl Reviews

Desperate Choices—Winner 2012 International Digital Award—Suspense

Desperate Choices—Best of Romance 2011 –Joyfully Reviewed

# DEDICATIONS AND ACKNOWLEDGEMENTS

A special shout out to all the readers who keep me going. I will admit there's no greater feeling in the world than bringing my characters to life and having readers not only identify with them, but want to be part of that world. I really wish Shiloh Springs, Texas, was a real place, because I want to live there.

To my sister, Mary. She is always there, helping me, encouraging me, and generally doing whatever it takes to get the writing done. Trust me, if she wasn't there prodding me, the books might never be finished.

And, as always, I dedicate this and every book to my mother, Betty Sullivan. She loved reading and shared her love for books with me at a young age.

**More about Kathy and her books can be found at**

**WEBSITE:**
**www.kathyivan.com**

**Follow Kathy on Facebook at**
**www.facebook.com/kathyivanauthor**

**Follow Kathy on Twitter at**
**twitter.com/@kathyivan**

**Follow Kathy at BookBub**
**bookbub.com/profile/kathy-ivan**

## NEWSLETTER SIGN UP

Don't want to miss out on any new books, contests, and free stuff? Sign up to get my newsletter. I promise not to spam you, and only send out notifications/e-mails whenever there's a new release or contest/giveaway. Follow the link and join today!

**http://eepurl.com/baqdRX**

# RIDGE

By
KATHY IVAN

# CHAPTER ONE

"How big is her property again?"

Ridge Boudreau sighed, rubbing a hand across his nape. He hated dealing with pencil pushers, especially ones who couldn't seem to remember information they'd been told a dozen times. Surely he had the information somewhere in all the files stacked on the table in front of him.

"Roughly twenty thousand acres. That's approximately thirty-one square miles," he added, before Roland Abernathy could ask. His boss, Daniel Kingston, shot him a sympathetic look and shrugged, as if to say "what're you gonna do?" Ridge and Daniel had worked together for several years, from the time Ridge was a rookie agent, learning the ropes of working with the Drug Enforcement Agency, taking down the nickel and dime dealers. He considered the man a good boss, easy to work with most of the time. Unless you screwed up. Then he'd hand you your head on a platter.

"And you're sure this Mary Margaret White knows about her property being used to run contraband, even condones it?" Roland pushed his glasses up on the bridge of his nose, blinking owlishly through the magnified lenses. "We can't afford to make a mistake. She's got the kind of money that she can hire the best lawyers in the country."

"That's why I'm going in undercover. Nobody's gonna swarm her property in a massive strike without proof. Besides, if she's a willing participant in drug running, we'll toss her backside into jail, same as the rest. I don't care how much money she's got; she's not above the law."

"Boudreau," Daniel sounded weary, which he probably was, considering he'd flown in on the redeye. "Are you positive we're looking in the right place? Her background doesn't suggest she'd put up with drug shipments running through her property."

"I've had geological surveys done of her place and the surrounding area. Most of it's still undeveloped wilderness. She's carved out about ten acres for her house and surrounding lawn, pool, stuff like that. The rest of it is unincorporated. We've done flyovers with high-tech drones and haven't seen anything unusual. But there are places where the trees are thick and obscure portions of the property. Without being able to go onto the land itself and search, we're working blind."

"Her file has some pretty big holes in it; otherwise, I'd say we could simply question her and her neighbors. But those holes make me think Ms. White might have something to hide. Boudreau, you know what to do. Survey the place, get chummy with the owner, and bring me proof. I'd like to exonerate her, if we can."

Ridge leaned back in his chair, studying his boss through hooded eyes. He'd swear the man looked like he'd aged ten years since the last time he'd seen him a few months previous. The lines around his mouth were deeper. The crow's feet around his eyes had nearly doubled, and there was a sallowness to his skin that worried him. *Could Daniel be sick?*

"If she's got nothing to hide, I'll be in and out, and we'll move on. Figure out where the trucks are disappearing to, because they are vanishing without a trace. I'm gonna figure it out."

"I know you will." Daniel stood and motioned for Roland, who made a mad scramble to gather all the papers and files he'd spread out on the tabletop. "We've rented rooms at a bed and breakfast. Got the last two rooms. We'll meet up there once you've got some intel. You sure you don't want me to bring the team in?"

Ridge stood and shoved his hands in his pockets, to keep from grabbing all Roland's papers and shoving them into his briefcase. Something about the guy got on his last nerve. This was only the second job he'd worked with him, and he hoped he'd manage to keep his cool, instead of mussing up the dude's perfectly styled hair or his shiny shoes. In a small town like Shiloh Springs, Roland stood out as a tourist with a capital T.

"Not yet. We'll keep this low key for now. If we

need 'em, I'll let you know. If too many people show up on Ms. White's land unannounced, she could slam a lid on her operation so tight it might take months, maybe even years, before we got another chance to bring it down."

"True. You sure your family doesn't know you're under-cover on a job this close to home?"

"I haven't told them anything. But most of my brothers are in law enforcement in one form or another, and they're smart. They won't blow my cover."

"I expect you to report in every twenty-four hours, got it?" Daniel's eyes narrowed and Ridge read the older man's determined expression. "No exceptions. I don't hear from you, the op is off and we're coming in."

"Twenty-four hours."

Ridge watched the two men, so different yet with the same end goal, walk out the front door of the coffee shop, pile into a nondescript sedan, and head back toward Shiloh Springs. Reaching into his wallet, he pulled out several bills, then added a couple more for a bigger tip. His fingers skimmed across the newspaper clipping he carried in his wallet, and he pulled it out, unfolded it, and studied the photo.

Mary Margaret White. The grainy black-and-white pho-to didn't do justice to the intelligence burning in her gaze as she stared out from the picture, or the quirk of her smile, lifting one corner of her mouth the tiniest bit higher than the other. She fascinated him. From the moment he'd heard mention of the possibility of trafficking so close to his home, he'd promised himself to find out who allowed drug shipments to cross their property, and put them away. And he would—even if it meant putting away Mary Margaret White. He knew his job, and he'd do it.

*Look out, Ms. White. I'm coming for you.*

Maggie moved the mouse with her right hand, staring at the display on her computer. *Well, sugar-foot.* The blips on her screen lit up like twinkle lights on a Christmas tree. Somebody was flying drones over her property. Again. Wasn't the first time. Her eyes narrowed as she studied the monitor, noting the almost grid-like pattern of the drones.

"That's it. You suckers are going down."

Shutting off the program, she marched to the closet by her front door and yanked it open, grabbing the shotgun and her hunting vest, the pockets already loaded with extra shells. Slamming her arms into the holes, she shrugged it on, and slapped her old straw hat on her head before storming out the front door.

After a quick sprint to the garage, she swung onto the seat of her Jeep, placing the shotgun on the passenger seat. She'd grown up with the Remington 870. Her daddy gave it to her when she was twelve. And like any good Southern girl, she took very good care of her guns. Speeding out of the garage, she headed down the gravel path leading away from her house and further into the densely wooded area beyond.

She had a pretty good idea what the drones were looking for, and she wasn't about to have her secret uncovered. Not now, and maybe not ever. It had taken a lot of hard work and money getting things exactly the way she wanted, and nobody with a fancy flying camera was undoing all her hard work.

She drove a couple of miles deep into her property before she pulled over and killed the engine. Closing her eyes and leaning her head back, she listened. The air was still and hot, without a breeze. Dead quiet, with no sound. Even the birds were silent. It seemed the entire forest held its breath, waiting. Long moments passed and still she heard nothing. Was she wrong? Could her computer program have a glitch and there really wasn't anything to see here?

Ah, wait. There it was. The sound she'd been listening for. The low hum increased, and she swung her legs out of the Jeep and jumped to the ground, reaching back inside for her Remington. Her baby, who never let her down, never missed. Tilting her head, she listened, focusing on the sound as it grew closer. She held her breath, remained perfectly still and for a long moment, all she heard was the pounding of her own heartbeat in her ears.

Lifting the shotgun to her shoulder, she positioned it at just the right angle, where it simply became an extension of her. Sighting her target, she slid her finger onto the trigger, gentle as a baby's caress and waited. Patience was the name of this game, and she had all the time in the world. Just a little bit closer and—

BAM!

The explosion of sound reverberated through the trees. Overhead, the frantic flapping of wings broke the stillness at the sharp echo of the gunshot, the leaves whipping around at the birds' flight. She couldn't contain her smirk as she watched the pieces of the drone scatter to the earth's floor, decimated and destroyed. There'd be no resurrecting that sucker. Standing over it, she plucked up a piece, and studied the ravaged hunk of metal and plastic.

"Hmm, that's interesting." Gathering the pieces scattered on the ground, she carefully piled them on the back seat of the Jeep. She'd take them home, study them. See if maybe they'd yield a clue as to who kept flying drones over her property. Then she would figure out a plan on stopping them.

On the way home, she took a circuitous route. There were rutted roads and pathways all over her property, many of them she'd intentionally widened enough for the Jeep to drive along. Others were little more than footpaths she could follow on horseback or with one of the motorcycles she kept for traversing her property.

She loved this land. It'd been in her family for decades, passed down through the generations, and now it belonged to her. It was ripe and fertile, the earth undisturbed for the most part, nurturing the natural flora and fauna, and she meant to keep it that way. More than one powerful city slicker had approached her family, wanting to buy up the land and build everything from strip malls to housing developments to a fancy resort. None of their offers had been received with anything but a resounding no thanks. She wasn't about to change that trend now.

Pulling into the garage, Maggie killed the engine and reached for the button to lower the door, but movement from the corner of her eye stopped her dead in her tracks. Somebody was sneaking around her property. Couldn't be Henry. She'd talked to him earlier that morning, and he'd asked for the day off. Felicia, her housekeeper, had already come and gone.

Reaching across the seat, she wrapped her hand around the shotgun and stepped out of the garage. Scowling at the thought of another trespasser, she skirted the perimeter of the house, eyes peeled for any sign of movement.

*Nothing.*

Was her imagination playing tricks on her? She got antsy ever since she'd caught a couple of up-to-no-good squatters on the back forty of her property, and chased them off. Why couldn't people mind their own business, and keep their noses out of hers?

There it was again. Somebody crept around the edge of her patio, although creeping might not be the best word. He really didn't slink or even try to hide. The way he walked reminded her of one of the bigger jungle cats. A lion or maybe a panther, all smooth, controlled muscle, coiled and ready to pounce.

With a moue of disgust, she flattened her back against the Texas limestone of her home and watched. Waited. And wondered what game the stranger was up to. He was far enough away she couldn't get a good look at his face, but the rest of him was a feast of sensuality. From his predatory walk to his dark hair, he exuded an almost feral nature. A wildness she'd never imagined being attracted to—until now.

His gaze seemed to miss nothing, studying not only the house, but the grounds. The flowering rose bushes she'd lovingly planted so long ago, when she'd first gotten married and life had been simpler. In hindsight, she could recognize the irony of planting roses. Her life had been nothing but prickly thorns for so long, she'd all but forgotten there was beauty to go along with the pain.

Some instinct must have alerted him, though she hadn't moved a muscle, because he stopped, frozen in place. He spread his hands out to his sides, palms forward, showing them to be empty. She knew he hadn't spotted her yet, but something made him realize he wasn't alone.

Lifting the shotgun, she stepped out into the open, and pointed it straight at him.

Never wincing.

Never flinching.

"I don't know who you are, and I really don't care. I've only got one thing to say." She hefted the gun higher, pointing it directly at his head. "Get off my property."

# CHAPTER TWO

It took every ounce of strength Ridge had to refrain from smiling. Dang, but his mark was cute. The gun was a nice touch, and she looked like she knew how to use it. Raising his hands slowly up to shoulder height, he kept his palms facing outward. No need to spook her. Her finger was way too close to the trigger.

"Ms. White?"

Her eyes narrowed at his use of her name. He took in every inch of her, from head to toe. Mary Margaret was dressed like a tomboy in jeans, a T-shirt that didn't hide a single one of her delicious curves, and a hunter's vest. A battered straw hat shaded a portion of her face, but what he could see matched the photo he carried in his wallet. Something about her called to him in a way no other woman ever had. He wanted to see her smile, to watch her eyes light up with desire. Taste her lips to see if they were as sweet as they appeared.

"I ain't buying whatever you're selling, Bub, so get back in your car and skedaddle."

*Skedaddle?*

"Alrighty. Guess I'll be on my way. Tell Henry I came by, and you kicked me off the property." He waited—one beat, two—and slowly lowered his hands as he turned, pretending he was going to leave. He made it all the way to four steps before she cracked.

"Wait."

Remaining faced away from her, he stopped. *Let her make the first move now. Retain the position of power.* He hoped her curiosity would overcome her initial reticence to discover why he'd shown up on her property, invaded her space. His cover story would hold—it always had, because for the most part, it was the truth. Sticking with the actual facts made it easier to maintain when deep undercover. He simply had to remember Mary Margaret White was his target, a suspect like any other suspect, no matter how pretty the outside package.

"You know Henry?"

Ridge turned around and faced Mary Margaret. His intel knew her friends called her Maggie, but he wasn't about to slip that little detail yet. One step at a time. Right now he had to bait the hook, get his little fishy caught and reeled in.

"We've known each other for several years. As a matter of fact, he's the one who called me. Asked me to meet him here."

"He's never mentioned you." The gun lowered, now pointed toward the ground, and he breathed a little easier. He didn't think she'd shoot him by accident. Nope, he got the impression she knew her way around guns, and if she did shoot him, it'd be deliberate and she wouldn't miss.

"Does Henry tell you about all his friends? Funny, he never really mentioned you at all. Except that he worked with you. Security."

"That's right."

"Which happens to be my area of expertise." Ridge motioned toward his shirt pocket, and after a few seconds, she nodded. Using two fingers, he pulled free a business card and held it out. "Henry called and asked me to come take a look around, see where things could be improved. Beef up what's in place, and discuss adding or upgrading your current situation."

She studied the card, before looking up and meeting his steady gaze. "Ridge Boudreau. Any relation to those Boudreaus over in Shiloh Springs?"

Ridge grinned at the way she said *those Boudreaus*. Not in a derogatory way, but more in a those-people-are-everywhere kind of way. Man, his momma would love Mary Margaret.

"Yes." Let her make what she would of his monosyllabic answer.

"I'm pretty sure Henry has the security around my home and property up-to-date. I doubt there's much you can do, Mr. Boudreau. Thanks, but no thanks."

Ridge raised his brow at her dismissal, though he wasn't surprised. Given the background the DEA's computer experts uncovered on Miss Mary Margaret—Maggie to her friends—White, she was justified in being leery of strangers. Hence the shotgun greeting.

"Your choice. But you might want to let Henry know you've got about a half dozen issues with the front gate and fencing at the entrance. Oh, and the sensors on your ground floor windows are inadequate. Those motion detectors could be disabled by a child. Egress through your kitchen is laughably inadequate. Thanks for your time, Ms. White."

"What? Wait a minute, Mr. Boudreau, I'll have you know I have top-of-the-line security, which is upgraded several times every year." The indignation written on her face was priceless, and exactly the response he'd expected. He'd sown the seed of doubt. Now he needed to play it cool, and let her take the initiative.

*Come on, little fishy, chomp on the hook, and I'm gonna reel you in.*

"I'm sure what you have is adequate for most homes. But are you looking for adequate? Henry told me you needed the best protection money could buy, and trust me when I tell you, right now what you've got wouldn't stop a determined person gaining access. For a professional? They'd barely break a sweat."

Ridge could practically see the wheels turning in her head, could almost predict what her next move would be—in fact, he was counting on it. He'd been doing this for a long time, though he didn't usually have to pull out the big guns, but he would. Rafe owed him a favor, and Ridge didn't have a problem calling it in.

"Ms. White, feel free to call the sheriff of Shiloh Springs. He can verify that I'm not only who I say, but that my credentials are legitimate. Although he might be a tad biased, since he's my brother. I can also give you the number for FBI Special Agent in Charge Derrick Williamson of the Austin office. I've worked with him on security issues in the past, and he can also verify my identity and my company's credentials."

"I'll do that, Mr. Boudreau."

He nodded and turned to leave, but couldn't resist one parting shot. "Give my best to Henry. Give me a call if you change your mind, and want me to take a deeper look at your security, Ms. White."

Without another word, he walked down the long drive and back toward the front gate. He knew she watched every step until he was out of sight of the house, and he finally relaxed and gave in to the laughter he'd suppressed. He'd been pleasantly surprised with Mary Margaret, maybe even a little shocked. She lived alone with only one security person and a housekeeper who came in for a couple hours every day. The rest of the time she stayed isolated on her ranch. Not an easy task for somebody who was filthy rich. He had expected to find a shy, timid woman who jumped at every shadow. Instead he found a firecracker, willing to challenge him on every level. And he found himself enchanted.

Climbing behind the wheel of his truck, he profoundly hoped she'd didn't turn out to be the mastermind behind one of the biggest drug-running operations in Central Texas.

# CHAPTER THREE

"Think she bought it?"

"Daniel, I know what I'm doing. Besides, I didn't lie. There really are several deficiencies in her security system. Duvall is doing a piss-poor job, if what she's got is any indication of his level of expertise."

Ridge sipped at his coffee. He'd left Mary Margaret's property and drove to the closest town, giving her some much needed time to call and verify his ID and his credentials. Rafe had already called back, saying she'd given him the fifth degree, checking out his story. Good thing he'd thought to give Rafe a heads-up yesterday. Once again, his instincts were proven correct. Now he wondered if she'd call Austin and grill Williamson about him.

"Just remember, Boudreau, we need you on that property ASAP. You need to find that route, and we need it closed now. Our informant called two hours ago. There's going to be another run going through in a week. So, unless we can catch them in the act, who knows how long we'll have to wait for the next shipment."

"Daniel, she's going to take the bait. I suspect I'll hear

from her before the day is over. You've got Henry ready to play his part, right? Because if he cracks and spills the story to her, it's over before we even get started."

"He's agreed. Swears there's no way anybody is running drugs across that property, and I believe he believes it. But if the security is as bad as you think, this guy might not even know what he's looking at when it's right under his nose."

"Think he'll keep the story straight?"

"We've gone over it a dozen times. He's gonna call her, tell her he's got a family emergency and has to go out of town for a little while. Once that's done, he's got a ticket to Maui on Uncle Sam's dime, as long as he keeps his mouth shut and doesn't contact Ms. White until the case is over."

"Do you trust him not to contact her? I got the impression he hangs around a lot."

"We've got somebody that'll be watching him twenty-four seven until we determine if Javier Escondido's pipeline is broken, and he's behind bars. Nobody wants to put this guy away more than me. I'm not taking any chances that Duvall will screw things up."

"She'll call. Probably sooner rather than later. I could see the wheels turning before I left, questioning where they'd screwed up. Though, I've got to admit, they did a lot of stuff right. There are a couple of places I probably couldn't access, not without a lot of time and specialized equipment."

"Always wondered why you decided to join the DEA with your background being security work. You've worked with some pretty highly placed clientele, and your references are topnotch. Ever gonna tell me?"

Ridge sighed. He knew Daniel had questions, though he'd been pretty good about not voicing them. Until now. "Maybe when this pipeline is shut down, we'll go out, have a few beers, and I'll tell you my sob story. Deal?"

"I'm gonna hold you to it, Boudreau. Now, I've got to go. Apparently, Ms. White is calling Henry."

Ridge couldn't hold back his grin. "Told ya."

"Jackass. Talk to you later."

Leaning back in his chair, Ridge took another sip of coffee.

"It shouldn't be long now."

Maggie dialed Henry's number, listening to the ringing and thinking about the tall, handsome stranger who'd shown up on her property. Something about him intrigued her. He didn't look like any security expert she'd ever seen. At a guess, she'd have pegged him as the criminal type, not the other way around.

His long dark hair had reached just past his shoulders, though he'd pulled it back into a low ponytail tied at his nape. It was dark, a rich, deep brown like strong coffee, though there were hints of blue-black in there, too. What had surprised her, though, was the startling blue of his piercing eyes. The combination of dark hair and light-colored eyes had always been her kryptonite. There was something about the startling contrast that made her heart skip a beat, but she'd never had a visceral reaction like she had with Ridge Boudreau. The second she set eyes on him, her heartbeat raced. Her breath caught in her chest until she felt lightheaded. An instantaneous attraction unlike anything she'd ever felt swept through her, and she'd wanted nothing more than to hear his voice. Touch his skin. Run her fingers through his shiny hair, see if it felt soft beneath her touch.

Henry answered on the fifth ring, right before it would have clicked over to voice mail. "Hey, Maggie."

"Listen, I need to ask you something. I—"

"Wait, Maggie, I need to tell you something."

Uh-oh. She didn't like the sound of that. There was something in his tone that immediately caused the little hairs on her arms to stand straight up. Whatever he had to say, it wasn't good news, of that she was sure.

"Okay, shoot."

"I have to go out of town for a little while. Not sure how long it's gonna be, and I hate leaving you in the lurch. I feel really bad, but there's a family situation and I gotta deal with it. I hope you understand."

"Of course I do. Anything I can do to help? Do you need anything? You know all you have to do is ask and it's yours."

She heard a soft sigh through the phone. "You're the best, Maggie. No, there's nothing you need to worry about.

I'm sure I can get things handled and I'll be back before you know it. It's just—I'm leaving today—this afternoon, as a matter of fact. But, I forgot to tell you, I made a call to a buddy. Name's Ridge Boudreau. He owns a security company, Sentinel Guardians, and trust me, he's really good at what he does. I asked him to come by your place, and take a look at the security we've got installed, and see if there are any upgrades we need to put into place. I meant to discuss it with you, but then I got called away, and now…"

"Mr. Boudreau already showed up, Henry. I'm afraid I wasn't at my most welcoming." She chuckled. "I pulled my Remington on him."

"You what?"

"The computer showed another drone doing a flyby, so I shot it down. Figured I'd see if we could determine where they're coming from. I think we both know what they're looking for. Anyway, I was on my way back to the house and I saw this stranger sneaking around, and I pulled my shotgun and demanded he get off my property."

Henry laughed. "I bet he loved that. And I doubt he was sneaking around, or you'd have never seen him."

"He left his card, and told me to check out his references. I talked to his brother, Rafe, who's the sheriff in Shiloh Springs. Gave him a glowing recommendation as being a law-abiding citizen and that his security services are legit. Course, him being his brother, I'm not sure how much stock I can put in that particular endorsement."

"He's definitely legit. I know he's done some government work."

"Yeah, he told me to contact the FBI office in Austin, said they'd attest to his qualifications."

"You know, Maggie, it wouldn't be a bad idea for Ridge to be there while I'm out of town. I know I'd feel better having somebody there with you, keeping an eye on things while I'm gone. He could fix any holes in our security, and be an unofficial bodyguard until I get back. Kill two birds kinda thing."

"I don't need a bodyguard. How many times do I have to tell you that?"

"Until the threats stop?"

"Jerk." She raked a hand through her hair, tucking it behind her ear. "It's not a good time for a stranger to be here, Henry. We're gonna have company in a couple of days, and I can't afford to have anybody sneaking around or snooping into my business. You know that."

"Figure out a way to keep Ridge occupied when you need him out of your hair. Trust me, Maggie, let him stay."

She leaned back against the kitchen barstool, and glanced through the huge window over the sink, loving the blue of the sky framed within its white border. Having Ridge around every day? It could be the biggest mistake of her life. But it also might be the chance to figure out if this instantaneous attraction between them could be…more.

"Alright. But if he steps one inch out of line, he's out on

his behind."

"Fair enough. Take care. I'll talk to you soon."

"Thanks, Henry. Don't forget to let me know if there's anything I can do. Bye."

Maggie disconnected the call, and leaned against the marble peninsula, her chin in her hand, wondering if she'd lost her ever-loving mind. Had she really just agreed to have a total stranger move into her house—her sanctuary? Ridge seemed a little too good to be true, and Maggie wasn't about to ignore her gut. She'd learned the hard way to never doubt her instincts, especially about men. Even with Henry's recommendation, she wanted a little more reassurance.

With a determined stride, she walked across the house to her office, and opened her laptop. Time to do a little research on Mr. Ridge Boudreau.

# CHAPTER FOUR

Ridge pulled his truck onto the wide circular driveway in front of Maggie's house, parked, and really looked at it. The day before, he'd done the usual cursory sweep, looking for security issues and areas where breaches could occur, but hadn't taken in the beauty of the home. The two-story house wasn't huge, probably a little over three thousand square feet, but it had an understated elegance that blended well with the rustic scenery. Texas limestone covered most of the outer walls, its pale color helping the structure blend into its surroundings. Not in a way to make it disappear so much as to help it seem like a natural extension of the land, as opposed to an artifice to man's desire to conquer.

The house suited Maggie's personality. There was the hint of a sharper edge that in no way detracted from its underlying unique beauty. While Maggie's outer appearance was lovely, Ridge had the feeling there was a lot more to her unplumbed depths, and he wouldn't mind digging a little deeper. Find out what had made and honed her into the spitfire he'd met the prior day.

Climbing from the truck, he grabbed his duffle from

behind the driver's seat and strode to the entrance. Double doors in a rich mahogany stood as a majestic entrance to the home. Lips quirking into a grin, he knocked. When no one answered, he wondered if Maggie had changed her mind about letting him stay. That wasn't gonna work, and she'd better get used to having him around, because he wasn't going anywhere.

Finally, one of the doors opened, and Maggie stood silhouetted in the opening, her hair pulled into a ponytail high on the back of her head, a towel draped around her neck. Sweat glistened on her shoulders, and her face shone with beads of perspiration. Workout gear of a tank top and shorts, along with athletic shoes gave away she'd been working out. Her cute little nose wrinkled when she spotted him on her doorstep.

"Well, don't just stand there. Come in."

"Yes, ma'am." Walking into the foyer, he loved the way the rest of the room opened into one large space, with huge floor to ceiling windows across the back of the house. Gleaming hardwood floors ran throughout the giant living area. A spotless kitchen on his left revealed sleek white cabinets with what looked like marble countertops, with stainless steel appliances that filled the space. In the center sat an enormous island. A peninsula to one side jutted out with bar stools lined up for casual dining. It was a gourmet chef's dream kitchen, and he couldn't help wondering how much of it Maggie actually used. Was she somebody who loved cooking or one of those people who barely knew their way around a microwave?

"Your room is down that hall on the right," she motioned. "Second door. Bathroom across the hall. Go ahead and put your things there, and help yourself to anything in the kitchen. Coffee's fresh. I'm gonna grab a shower. Be back in a few."

Spinning on her heel, she headed down another hall past the kitchen and disappeared from sight. With a shrug, he checked out his room, leaving the duffle beside the door. After a quick glance around the other bedrooms in his wing of the house and doing a quick assessment of the security already in place, he headed toward the kitchen. Pouring himself a cup of coffee, he wandered over to the tall glass windows, and looked at the back of the home.

The patio looked like something out of a high-end magazine. The patio was covered with a large lanai, with enough seating to comfortably seat several. An outdoor kitchen contained a state-of-the-art grill, a built-in refrigerator, and a wine cooler. An enormous in-ground pool dominated a huge portion of the yard. He grinned, imagining diving into the cool, crisp depths at the end of a long day, listening to the waterfall gurgling in the background. Maybe some soft music played softly through the speakers he spotted around the grotto-like area at one end of the pool.

"Did you get settled in?" Maggie stood beside him, a matching mug in her hand. "If there's anything you need, let me or Felicia know. She's my housekeeper. She comes every morning, so if you don't see her, leave a note on the kitchen counter, and she'll find it."

"I'm sure I've got what I need, or I can have one of my team bring me anything. Don't worry."

"Team?"

"Depending on how big or small a job is, I have a few people who work with me. They are qualified in different areas of security expertise, and do a lot of the hands-on work. Running cables, digging trenches, crawling around in attics and basements, that sort of thing."

Maggie smiled. "So, they do all the dirty work, and you stand back and take the credit."

Ridge chuckled. "Not exactly. I don't have a problem getting my hands dirty."

She took a sip of her coffee. "Henry spoke highly of your expertise. Your brother sang your praises. Tell me, Mr. Security Expert, about some of the changes you think I need."

"I'm going to want to do a complete walkthrough of your current system, all the electronics, programs you've got installed, a map of your property and what you've already got covered and what you'd like covered. And a list of any people allowed access to the property, whether you have had any unauthorized people accessing your property without your consent. It'll help me gauge what's working and what's not." He paused, watching her face for any signs of distrust or disbelief. "For starters, though, the leads on your lower story windows need a serious upgrade. Anybody who's seen current movies or TV can figure out how to disrupt the connection without triggering the alarms."

"How? Not that anybody's tried, but when they were installed, I was assured they were nearly foolproof. Are you saying they lied?"

Ridge shook his head slowly. "Not lied necessarily. More like sold you something that wasn't the latest upgrade. When were those installed?"

"I'd have to look up the exact dates, but maybe three years ago." She got a faraway look in her eyes, and whatever thought crossed her mind wasn't pleasant, that much Ridge could tell. Almost immediately, she masked her expression, but not before he'd read the pain in her eyes, and the tightening of her lips. He'd need to find out what happened three years earlier to cause that sort of knee-jerk reaction.

"Mind if I take a closer look at them? If I'm right, which of course I am," he teased, "the brand of sensor might be the problem."

"Be my guest," she motioned toward the windows on either side of the front door. "Let's take a look."

She trailed behind him, stooping down beside him when he squatted to look at the window frame. Studying the small item attached to the frame, he grinned. He loved it when he was right.

"It's what I thought. This particular brand has an inherent flaw in its design. It was pulled from the market about eighteen months ago by the manufacturer. You should have been notified at the time with an offer to do an upgrade on the actual connector."

Maggie studied each area he pointed to, her head cocked to the side. Shaking her head, she glared at him. "I didn't get anything. Which really annoys me, especially with as much money as this whole system cost me. How do we fix this?"

Ridge's gut tightened at her use of the word *we*. It was only a tiny step, but it meant she'd started to listen, to trust him.

"It's a fairly straightforward fix. I'll get the right parts ordered today." He straightened and held out his hand. Maggie stared at it for a second, then two, before sliding hers into it. A surge of awareness shot through him at her touch.

"I'd like to take a look at your inhouse computer system, see what programs you're using. Check out what software you have, and make suggestions for anything you might be missing or that you should intensify."

"Follow me."

He walked a step or two behind her, watching her hips sway with each step. There was an inherent grace about her movements, a sensuality underlying every move. He doubted she was even aware of it, but his every instinct screamed to attention as he watched her. Reminded himself he needed to be on his toes and not fall under her spell. She might be a gorgeous seductress, but he had a job to do, and a drug pipeline to shut down. The job came first—it had to. There was no other option.

Walking past the master bedroom, he couldn't resist taking a quick glance through the open doorway. Soothing teals, aquas, and splashes of orange and bronze popped on the walls and bedding. His lips quirked up at the sight of the king-sized bed dominating a good portion of the room.

He quickened his step as Maggie turned into a doorway just past the master bedroom, and stepped inside what appeared to be another bedroom that had been converted into an office space. A large, U-shaped desk overshadowed the smaller room, with several flat-screen monitors nearly overwhelming the available desk space.

"Henry usually manages all these computer systems, though I know how to use it. This one," she pointed to one of the monitors currently displaying split screens, "is focused on the front gate and entrance to the property. This one covers the back of the house, including the pool area and patio."

"Good. I'll take a look at those. What's this one?" he asked, pointing to a screen showing a weird grid-like pattern. He leaned in closer, trying to determine if the program was what he thought. Because if it was, that could cause some serious problems.

Maggie grinned like a proud parent. "That's my new toy. It's not on the market yet."

Ridge folded his arms across his chest, and stood with his

feet spread apart. "It's a D28-Arrow?"

"You've heard of it?"

"What I'd like to know is how you got your hands on one."

"I know a guy who knows somebody in research and development. He was able to get me a prototype." Maggie shoved her hands into the back pockets of her jeans, and Ridge had to blink twice before his brain started working again. Dang, she was cute, especially when she grinned like that.

"I've heard of it." Now it was his turn to grin. "Matter of fact, I know the inventor personally. I even helped work out a few of the bugs." And Gizmo was going to get an earful about letting somebody on his R&D team smuggle a copy of the software off-site.

"Seriously? It's so cool. Matter of fact, that's what I was doing yesterday when I found you here. It spotted a drone flying over my property, and I tracked it. Shot the sucker down."

"You shot down a drone? How'd you continue to track it after you left the house?" Far as he knew, last time he'd talked to Gizmo, that capability was still a long way off.

"Err…I probably shouldn't tell you. Since you know the inventor, and I don't want to get my source in trouble."

Ridge ran his hand through his hair, and counted to ten. "Ms. White—"

"Maggie. If you're going to be living with me, you might

as well call me Maggie."

There it was—he'd been hopeful she'd trust him enough to let him call her by the nickname, and he felt a surge of satisfaction. It hadn't taken nearly as long as he'd anticipated.

"Maggie, I'm not trying to get you or your friend in trouble. I'd really like to know how you managed to track the drone. Last I heard, it was still being done by someone staying at the computer, while a second person did the outdoor tracking, communicating via cell phones."

"I…well…I wrote an app."

"You what?" Ridge thought he'd kept the incredulous tone out of his voice, but apparently not, because her eyes narrowed, and her back stiffened.

"I'm not a complete idiot, Mr. Boudreau. I even managed to graduate high school and everything."

"Maggie, I'm sorry. I never meant to imply anything. I'd like to know what you did, and maybe pass that information along to the man who wrote the program. He's been working on figuring out a viable solution to being able to follow a drone without visible confirmation and sight lines. Being able to walk away from the indoor computer, go out into the field and know exactly where the drone is, follow it, trust me, that's a huge breakthrough for his software."

"I walked through the program backward, starting from the moment the blip shows. Tracing the steps, I converted the angles, longitude, latitude, and using an algebraic equation, I wrote an app. It's not perfect, and only gets me within ten to fifteen yards, but once I'm that close, I can usually stand still and listen, figure out which direction the motorized sound is coming from."

"We're talking an app, like you'd download onto a tablet or cell phone? Man, Gizmo's gonna have a heart attack when he hears somebody beat him to the punch. Mind giving me a copy of your programming?"

Her eyes narrowed before she asked, "Who's Gizmo?"

Ridge chuckled. "Sorry, Gizmo is the man who invented D28-Arrow. Guy's a certified genius."

"Gizmo—sounds like some kid down in his mom's basement, hacking into government servers, not developing high-tech spyware."

"He's definitely not a kid. Friend of my dad's, they were in the Army together. Got the nickname in the field, when he could take apart and put together just about anything they threw at him. When he left the Army, he started tinkering with things on his own, and managed to create a few things for Uncle Sam, and a few others for the private sector. When I say he's a certified genius, I mean that in the literal sense. Guy's got a MENSA-level IQ. And he's gonna have kittens when he sees what you've done with his baby."

"Okay, I'll make you a copy."

"Now, about this drone you shot down. I take it this wasn't the first one you've had, or you wouldn't have needed D28-Arrow. Got a problem with drones?"

Maggie nodded. "Not at first, but over the last few months, I'm getting more and more, flying over the entire property. Didn't think much about them at first. I figured it was just kids getting new toys, showing off for their friends, that kind of thing." He watched a shadow cross her face, as she fell silent. Made a mental note to ask her about it later, because it was obviously upsetting her to talk about.

"You shot one down. Can I take a look at it?"

"Sure, though you're not gonna find much info. No markings, nothing to identify who made it, or where it came from."

Ridge knew the DEA had suggested flying drones over the property a couple of times, but not in the last few days. They'd tried a couple initially, but due to the dense tree growth, they'd discarded that pretty quickly. Now he was curious to see if the DEA had decided to try again, or if somebody else was interested in Maggie's activities.

"Who knows? I'm a naturally curious sort, I'd still like to take a look."

She pointed to a box sitting on a fold-up TV tray. "Knock yourself out."

"Thanks." Walking over, he sifted through the drone's wreckage, lifting out one or two pieces, studying them, before tossing them back into the box. Nope, wasn't one of theirs.

"I'll print you a map of the land, the boundaries, and where alarms and sensors are placed. Anything else you need, give me a shout. Now, I'm hungry, I haven't had breakfast yet. You want some?"

He gave her a lopsided grin. "I'd love some."

Tossing her ponytail over her shoulder, she headed out the door and back toward the kitchen, Ridge trailing along like a housebroken puppy. Things definitely weren't boring at Maggie White's house, and it looked like he'd have his hands full figuring out whether good ole Maggie was as sweet and sassy as she seemed, or if she was a monster.

# CHAPTER FIVE

M aggie e-mailed a copy of her app's schematics to Ridge, who said he'd make sure Gizmo knew she wasn't trying to hack his software and steal his baby. Which was never her intent. She'd simply found what she considered a glitch, and found a solution. It's what she did, the way her mind worked.

"Maggie, I left a roast with potatoes and carrots cooking in the crockpot on the counter. There's a salad in the fridge, and rolls are rising in the warming drawer. Just stick 'em in the oven right before you're ready to serve dinner, and you should be good to go."

Felicia Gaines leaned her hip against the marble countertop, and watched Maggie's face expectantly. Maggie knew the other woman desperately wanted to find out why Ridge was staying in the guest room. As much as Maggie wanted to confide in her friend, there was only one problem. Felicia was one of the biggest blabbermouths she knew, and it wouldn't take long before everybody in town would hear that Maggie was shacking up with a tall, dark, and delicious stranger.

"Thanks, Felicia." She bit back a grin, and silently began her mental countdown. Three, two, one, and…

"Come on, Mags, don't do this to me. Spill. Who is that gorgeous hunk of handsomeness? What's he doing here in the middle of tiny town Texas? Are you two an item or what? Is he single? Available? Please say he's available and looking for a good time. Please…"

Maggie looked at her dearest friend, standing with her hands folded in front of her in supplication, begging for answers, and burst into laughter. "His name is Ridge Boudreau."

Felicia's eyes widened at Ridge's last name. Unless they lived under a rock, everybody within a hundred-mile radius had heard of the Boudreaus.

"Boudreau—as in the Shiloh Springs Boudreaus? Girl, I didn't know you knew them personally."

"I don't *know them* know them. I met him yesterday."

"Oh, tell me everything. Was it an instant attraction? When your eyes met, was it all swoon-worthy? Did you go all weak in the knees? Because, girlfriend, he's gorgeous."

"Nothing like that. I didn't know he was coming. When we first met, I pulled a gun on him."

"What! No way! Are you serious?"

"As a heart attack. He scared the living daylights outta me. I had no clue who he was. He was just some guy sneaking around the side of the house, and I had the shotgun with me, so I kinda told him to get his backside off my land."

Felicia sputtered, covering her mouth with her hands to hold in her laughter. "I can picture it. You've always had a bit of a *take no prisoner* attitude. Bet he didn't back down though, right?"

"Yep. Turns out he knows Henry. Apparently, Ridge is a security expert, and Henry asked him for a second opinion on upgrading my system. Only he didn't bother telling me Ridge was coming."

"Oh, a suspenseful first meeting. Doesn't explain what he's doing staying here, though. I saw his bag when I was cleaning, which means he's planning on spending the night."

Maggie drew in a deep breath before answering. "He's going to be sticking around for a few days, while Henry's out of town."

"Well, I for one am glad he'll be around for a few days." Felicia swiped a kitchen towel across the peninsula's top, a halfhearted gesture at best. "I don't like the thought of you being out here alone. Even with all your fancy security, I can't help worrying." She grinned, her expression filled with glee. "Maybe I could stay for a few days. We could have a couple of days of lying around the pool in our bikinis, sipping margaritas, and watching Mr. Sexy do his thing."

Maggie rolled her eyes at the suggestion. "Nope. You've got work, and I'm busy."

Felicia sighed and tossed the kitchen towel at Maggie's head. She caught it before it landed, and flung it back.

"You're always busy lately. I miss spending time with you. Shoot, we haven't had a girls' night out in forever."

It was true. Maggie had dug herself in so deep in her secret project, she'd neglected everything else in her life. Walking over to Felicia, she gave her a hug.

"I'm sorry. I know I've been preoccupied. Honestly, I didn't mean to make you feel like I was ignoring you. I promise, as soon as I can, we'll do something. Maybe take a long weekend, and go down to South Padre Island, and lie on the beach and soak up some rays. Okay?"

"Promise?" Guilt swept through Maggie at the wistful appeal in her friend's voice.

"My word of honor. Now, you've got to get to your class, and I need to see what Mr. Boudreau is up to."

Felicia waggled her brows, making Maggie chuckle. "You sure you don't want me to stick around? I'd love to help watch Mr. Boudreau work. I'm really good with my hands, ya know. I could assist him in all kinds of ways."

"I'll be sure to pass your offer along. Now, scoot. I'll see you in a couple days."

"Seriously, Mags, if you need anything, give me a shout. I can be back in around thirty minutes."

"I know, and I appreciate it."

Felicia walked to the closet by the front door and grabbed her purse hanging on the hook, and dug out her car keys.

Watching her friend go, Maggie smiled and headed toward her bedroom. She had a couple things she needed to check on, and while Ridge was working with the computer system in her office, now would be the perfect time. Especially since she didn't want or need him butting into her private affairs. Things might get a little dicey with Henry out of the picture for a few days, but she could handle things on her own.

She'd been handling things on her own for a long time.

Ridge looked into the cardboard box containing the remains of the drone Maggie shot down, and decided to ship it off to Gizmo. Have him take a look at it, see if he could figure out where it came from, who it might belong to, since there were no markings he could see to identify it. The small engine was damaged. Obviously, Maggie was a darn good shot with that shotgun of hers.

Hearing a noise down the hall, he walked over to the doorway, and spotted Maggie heading out of her bedroom. She'd changed into a pair of jeans that hugged her curves, and a long-sleeved shirt with a high neck. Boots encased her feet, and he smiled, noting they were the prerequisite cowboy boots that everybody, man and woman alike, favored in Texas. Her hair was pulled back into a long tail, restrained at the back of her neck with a large clip.

Her purposeful stride away from him aroused his curiosity, and he couldn't help wondering where she was headed. Following her felt like an invasion of her privacy, but he couldn't afford to give her that luxury. The job took precedent over the illusion of freedom, and he quietly followed her, his footsteps soundless against the hardwood floors.

Watching her pull that battered straw hat from the closet, he knew she planned on leaving the house. There was no way he was staying behind. Not when he had the perfect opportunity to see what she was up to, because there wasn't a doubt in his mind Maggie had secrets. It was his job to uncover them.

Staying a few feet behind and out of sight, he followed. She never spotted him, never looking left or right, but headed straight for the huge garage. Within a couple of minutes, he watched an older Jeep pull out, and he silently cursed. He'd thought to follow her on foot, not realizing she meant to travel any great distance. Though he might be able to catch up to her in his pickup, there was no way she wouldn't spot him.

Slapping his cowboy hat against his thigh, he walked back to the house. Might as well check in with Daniel and update him. At least the first part of their plan worked; he was staying in her house.

He headed for the office, and watched the monitors, scanning each covered location, hoping for a glimpse of Maggie's Jeep. Curiosity roused, he couldn't help wanting to know where she'd headed. Who she was meeting up with? Was it her contact with the cartel? His gut clenched at the thought of her being involved in this mess. There was an innocence about her, a sweetness of spirit that he couldn't imagine being corrupted by the ugliness of drug runners and their dirty money, pedaling their deadly concoctions.

Eyes glued to the monitors, he pressed the button and dialed Daniel's number.

"Boudreau, talk to me."

"We're in."

"Excellent work. She bought your cover story?"

"Absolutely. I'm staying onsite and right now, I'm studying her security setup. I've got a good view of the house and the surrounding area, but I'm not seeing any video farther out than the back forty. I'll have to spend some time exploring the wooded areas, look for the road the smugglers are using."

"I was hopeful we'd be able to spot it from the security feeds. Can you add additional cameras?"

"Would take way too long. I'm going to open a link so Buckeye can monitor the system remotely. That way, we can keep eyes on the monitors that we do have twenty-four seven, without Maggie being aware of our presence."

"Maggie?"

"Mary Margaret. She prefers to be called Maggie."

Daniel sighed. "Boudreau, don't get too chummy with the suspect. That's a complication we can't afford."

"Look, I know how to do my job, and I'll work whatever angle I need to take down these scum-sucking dealers and put their bosses behind bars, and get that crap out of the hands of kids. If that means getting...closer to Maggie White, it's all part of the job."

"Fine, fine. This is your op. What've you found so far?"

"Before we get to that, do you know anything about drones flying over the property? Did you authorize anything and forget to tell me?"

"Not recently. You know we did a few flyovers a couple weeks back, but the foliage is far too dense to get anything useful. Did some satellite surveillance too, but for the most part, that was a bust. Found a couple places where it looked like vehicles could drive through, but when we checked them out, they petered out to nothing but scraggly footpaths." Daniel's voice trailed off, before he sputtered. "Are you telling me somebody's flying drones over her land?"

Ridge chuckled. His boss hated being in the dark about anything concerning an ongoing investigation. "It appears somebody has been flying low-level drones. Maggie managed to blow one outta the sky yesterday."

"She what?"

"You heard me. I studied what remained after taking a shotgun blast, but I can't find any markings to indicate who or where it came from. I'm gonna send it to somebody who might be able to get us answers."

"I can pick it up, have it sent to—"

"Don't bother. My guy can get me the answers faster and keep the information under wraps."

"Does he have clearance? We can't send anything out without authorization unless they've got clearance."

"Trust me, Gizmo's clearance is higher than mine or yours. We're covered on that front."

"Fine. What else have you got?"

Ridge explained about the security set up, not mentioning Maggie owning a copy of D28-Arrow. That information would send Daniel into palpitations. Instead, he explained what she had, the progress he'd made with gaining her trust, and the pros and cons of upgrading her system.

"Let the guys know I'm gonna call 'em in to do a couple of installs, once I convince Maggie they're needed. They'll keep her occupied, freeing me up to survey the lay of the land. I mean to find that pipeline and destroy it, Daniel."

"I know. It's just as important to me, too. Keep me up-to-date, and let me know what this Gizmo person finds out about the drone."

"Will do."

Hanging up, Ridge leaned back in his chair, hands behind his head, and wondered what secrets Maggie was hiding. He'd have to up his game if he wanted to catch Ms. Maggie in the act. A self-satisfied smile lifted the corners of his mouth.

"Let the games begin."

# CHAPTER SIX

M aggie sat inside the Jeep and studied the overhead canopy stretched out underneath the upper branches of the treetops. It was anchored in place on the four corners to each trunk, spreading it out to camouflage the area below from prying eyes. She'd taken the precaution after she'd discovered the satellite surveillance photos showed everything beneath the widespread branches was clearly visible to the prying electronic eye in the sky.

The netting was military grade, with lifelike leaf structures attached to blend seamlessly into its surroundings. Hanging the suckers had been a chore, one she'd done herself, because she hadn't trusted anybody else with the job. Keeping this area hidden away from prying eyes was too important to leave in the hands of somebody who might talk—if the price was right.

The camo netting was anchored high off the ground, making it hard to spot unless you stood directly beneath it and looked up. Otherwise, it simply blocked out the light from below, and blocked the ground from view from above. So far, it was working.

She put the Jeep in park in front of the small trailer parked beneath the trees, in the area she'd had cleared months earlier, when she'd decided on her course of action. One she didn't have a single regret about making. The tiny home was barely six hundred square feet, well self-contained for short-term usage, small enough for somebody to escape to for a few hours or a few days without anybody noticing.

On either side stood two identical tiny houses on wheels, painted in shades of tan, brown and green, helping them blend into their surroundings, much like the camo netting above them. Currently, all three were unoccupied, though that would change in a few days, when the truck came through.

Climbing the two steps, she went inside, her eyes scanning for any disturbance. Sometimes a critter or two managed to get inside, and she'd have to roust them. So far, so good. Opening the single upper cabinet above the tiny cook stove, she grabbed the small notebook from her back pocket, and began inventorying the supplies, noting what needed to be replaced. Having enough foodstuffs in each cabin and emergency supplies necessary for a comfortable survival, had been a learned response, one she never wanted to forget.

Checking under the sink, she noted she was low on bottled water and marked to pick up a couple of cases for each house. Since the houses didn't have running water, making sure there was plenty on hand was not a luxury, it was a necessity. Composting toilets took care of other critical needs.

She needed to get a new mattress for the house on the left. This one was wearing thin and ragged in spots, but for now it would have to do; she didn't have time to get one ordered. Walking back out to the Jeep, she grabbed the bucket with her cleaning supplies and headed into tiny home number one. It didn't take long to do a fairly thorough cleaning, dusting and refreshing it until the surfaces sparkled. The other two followed in quick order, and before long she'd finished sprucing up all three.

Placing the supplies onto the floor of the Jeep, she climbed behind the wheel, and headed back home. Most of the time, she took different paths to get to the tiny houses. But today, she'd have to make a run into town to stock up on the depleted food supplies, and drove straight back to her house. Pulling into the garage, she climbed out of the Jeep and noticed Ridge standing in the garage door opening.

"Hey."

"Have fun?"

There was something about the low growl, the way the words were deep and rough, that caused her to pause before answering.

"Something wrong, Ridge?"

He sighed. "No. Just frustrated. I worked on the drone for a bit, trying to figure out where it might be from, but no luck. If it's okay, I'd like to send it to Gizmo. They might be able to get something off the motor to figure out where it was made, or a way to figure out who's flying it over your property."

"I'm okay with that. I'd like to know who's spying on me."

He leaned against the doorjamb and crossed his arms over his chest. "Spying? That's an odd choice of words. You have something to hide, Maggie?"

"Not really. I would like to know what they are searching for. They could simply call and ask me. Or knock on the door if it's that important."

Ridge's smile was instantaneous. "And would you greet them the way you did me, at the end of your shotgun?"

Maggie found herself smiling in turn. "Nope. You're a special case, Ridge."

His gaze immediately turned heated, and Maggie felt the blood rush into her cheeks at his perusal. "And don't you forget that, Miss Maggie." Reaching forward, he ran his knuckle softly against her cheek, and her eyelids lowered, shielding her gaze. "What have you been up to this fine morning?"

"Not much," she whispered, swallowing to clear her throat. "Had a couple errands to run. I'm going to make a run into town soon. Anything you need?"

"Mind if I tag along?"

Her head jerked up. "Why? I thought you were working on the security issues."

"I am. I've got a couple of things to pick up, and I'm meeting with one of my crew. He'll be coming out tomorrow to begin installing those sensors I mentioned yesterday. He was able to find some in Austin, and he's going to drive over there today and pick them up."

"Oh. Sure, I mean…I'm leaving in about half an hour." She walked past him, and then glanced back over her shoulder. "Don't be late, or you'll get left behind."

"Don't you worry, Miss Maggie, I'll be here."

With that parting shot, he walked around the corner of the garage and disappeared toward the back of the house. Maggie watched him walk away, felt the hitch in her breathing, and knew she was in so much trouble. Ridge didn't seem to miss a thing, and keeping secrets from a man who made a living looking for loopholes might be her undoing.

# CHAPTER SEVEN

Maggie pulled her car into the parking lot of the supermarket, and turned in the seat to face him. Ridge had let her drive, figuring she needed the illusion of controlling the situation. She'd seemed a bit off-kilter the rest of the morning before they'd headed into town, and letting her appear in charge of her portion of the world was such a minor thing. Following her lead might prove interesting, though he wouldn't hang onto her coattails. He had Rabbit for that.

He'd worked a couple jobs with Rabbit before and been impressed. The guy was sharp, blended into the background like a chameleon, and he was fast. Like supersonic fast on his feet. The members of his DEA team were already assembled and assimilated into town. They'd shown up over the past couple of days, scouted out the lay of the land in and around the outskirts, and set up a basic command center at the largest hotel. It wasn't anything fancy, one of those chain places where you tended to blend into the background. Part of the team was staying there, while the rest picked an innocuous motel, splitting the team between the two locations. No sense alerting anybody that a bunch of out-of-towners had hunkered down in their burb. A quick text before he'd left Maggie's house had Rabbit ready to follow her wherever she went. Ridge meant to keep tabs on her without being too close. It wouldn't do to rouse her suspicious, not when he had basically gotten free rein of her place.

"What's the plan?"

She picked up her phone from the middle console, and swiped her finger across the screen. "I need to hit up the grocery store for some supplies. Shouldn't take long."

He nodded, staring out the windshield. "Great. I'm meeting up with a client. Text me when you're ready to head back."

"Alright." She drawled out the word, like she'd been expecting something different from him. Good. Keeping her on her toes, trying to figure him out, seemed a good play. If he wasn't nipping at her heels, maybe she'd slip up and reveal her plans via Rabbit's surveillance. When he'd checked out the Jeep earlier, there'd been fresh mud caked on the tires, so wherever she'd headed off to in such a hurry hadn't been on paved roads. The fact that she was hiding something, while suspicious, mostly aroused his curiosity. Nothing Ridge liked more than a good puzzle, and in Maggie he'd found the perfect riddle.

Climbing from the car, he gave her a quick wave and strode away, deliberately not looking back, though he felt her eyes watching his retreating form. In his hand, he carried the box containing the ravaged drone. He planned on meeting up with Daniel, and having him ship it to Gizmo. Daniel was also bringing him a couple of GPS trackers to place on Maggie's car and her Jeep. He felt a bit guilty planting the bugs, but regrets wouldn't get the job done and find the pipeline and the smugglers.

Walking through the doors of the coffee shop, he spotted his boss sitting at a small round table at the back. After placing his order for a large black coffee, he headed over, easing onto a chair. Daniel had a cup sitting in front of him. Roland sipped on one of those frou-frou coffee drinks, the kind with all the whipped cream on top. Ridge barely refrained from rolling his eyes.

Roland had no business being out in the field. He was great with numbers and all the finite details of his team's behind the scenes activities. In the real world, where DEA agents put their lives on the line every day, the citified accountant stood out like the proverbial sore thumb.

He laid the box on the table and pushed it toward Daniel. "Here's the drone we talked about. Get it to Gizmo ASAP. Shouldn't take him long to get answers on who's spying on Maggie's property."

Roland perked up at the sight of the box. "A drone?"

"Not one of ours," Ridge shot back.

When his name was called, Ridge stepped away long enough to grab his coffee, flashing a smile at the young girl behind the counter, who blushed, before he headed back to his seat.

"You have what I asked for?" His boss tossed him a small plastic bag, containing the GPS tracking devices. Ridge pocketed them, and then took a sip of his coffee.

Daniel shot a glare toward Roland, who kept picking at the tape on the package holding the drone, before turning his attention back to Ridge. "Anything new? Other than somebody flying drones over her place?"

"Maggie snuck out of the house this morning. Drove off before I could catch her. I'm pretty sure she didn't leave the property. She wasn't gone long enough. And her tires were caked with mud. If she'd stuck to the public roads, which are paved, she wouldn't have picked up anything."

"You think she was meeting somebody? Maybe about the shipment?" Excitement laced Daniel's voice.

"Don't know. I'm going to spend a couple of hours later tonight checking the lay of the land, after she's gone to bed. Can't do it before, or she'd be suspicious. There's only so much tap dancing I can do without giving the game away. A security specialist works within the house and outlying structures, not gallivanting around the property. I might get away with suggesting perimeter fencing, but anything more and it's gonna raise eyebrows."

"Gallivanting?" Roland snickered and Ridge barely resisted another eye roll. Why had Daniel brought this guy along?

"Get those trackers on her vehicles ASAP." Daniel slammed his fist on the tabletop. "I want her every movement monitored. She's our number one suspect. We have to shut off the route. Allowing the drivers to get off the interstate where we've got a higher saturation of agents, they've doubled what's gotten through over the past six months."

"How sure are we they're using Maggie's land to move the drugs? I mean, there are other good-sized pieces of unincorporated, undeveloped properties in the area. Not nearly as big as hers, but cutting a swath across unoccupied land? Could be happening someplace else, right?"

Something still didn't sit right in Ridge's gut about this whole situation. After having met Maggie, spent a little time with her, he couldn't picture the dark-haired beauty consorting with smugglers.

"Ridge, we've been over this before. Ms. White's property is the perfect place for larger vehicles to drive across without being spotted. It's far enough off the interstate to not arouse suspicion, and has huge areas of acreage with large native foliage which provides natural camouflage. There is access to paved roads bordering it on both the north and the south. Our biggest problem has been gaining access without going through official channels, because then the property owner is informed. If they are involved in the smuggling, it blows our chance at catching the smugglers red-handed. And two, finding a drivable path through such densely forested land is a daunting task, because the foliage from above makes it nearly impossible to survey by satellite. I'll be honest, until you brought this," he motioned toward Gizmo's package, "I never considered using drones again. We have satellite images, but they're practically useless because of the dense forestation. Our sources are credible, and they point at Ms. White not only being involved, but culpable in providing access to her land, and right-of-passage to the drug smugglers."

Ridge shook his head, refusing to believe Maggie was involved. He'd be the first to admit he didn't know her well enough to be one hundred percent positive, but after spending time with the woman, he'd willingly risk his reputation with the DEA that she was innocent.

"I'll try and get the trackers on her vehicles today or tomorrow, depending on when she's around. I'll tag the ones she uses the most, though she's got several really nice cars and trucks in her garage."

"I don't care how you get them on, just get it done." Daniel ran a hand through his hair, a gesture Ridge was all too familiar with. His boss did it whenever he got frustrated, or thought a case was turning sideways.

"I'm sorry you're spending so much time away from your family, boss. How're June and Sammy?"

"Not happy that I haven't been home in months. Sam's started playing Little League, and I've missed every stinking practice. June says he's being a good sport about it, understands that Daddy's working. But I hate it. I want to be there to see his first at-bat. I should be in the stands, cheering him on, watching him play second base. Instead, I'm sitting here in a coffee shop in Texas Hill Country, trying to take down a Mexican drug cartel."

"Hopefully, it'll all be over soon, and we'll have thrown a huge monkey wrench into Escondido's pipeline. You'll get a break, and be sitting on the sidelines at your son's games before you know it. All I ask is you send me pictures."

Daniel pulled out his phone, tapped a couple of buttons, and turned the phone toward Ridge. "June took this one last week."

Ridge whistled low. "I almost don't recognize the kid. Man, he's growing so fast."

"Yeah, and I've missed too much of it." Daniel tucked his phone into his jacket pocket, and placed his hands on the table. "Everybody knows what their assignments are. The teams are in place. I'll get the drone to your buddy Gizmo. Keep looking for where the trucks are cutting through. I've got a couple of guys patrolling the roads to the north and south of Ms. White's property, doing surveillance for anybody looking suspicious."

Ridge stood when Daniel did, while Roland gathered up the various pads, papers and pens he'd spread over the tabletop. "I'll check in tonight after I've searched, either by text or e-mail."

"My gut tells me we're close. We can't afford to make

any mistakes." Daniel's expression hardened. "I got word this morning that the heroin confiscated from the last Escondido bust was laced with fentanyl. He's getting dangerous and careless. Who knows how many people died from that poisonous combination?"

Shock coursed through Ridge at his boss' words. If Escondido's crew was lacing their product with fentanyl, that ramped up the urgency tenfold. Fentanyl had become the latest rage for users, because the high and the rush it gave magnified anything heroin alone produced. But it was also deadly.

"I've got to get back, Maggie's gonna be waiting for me." He gave Daniel a brisk nod. "We'll get them."

Without another word, Ridge walked out into the sunshine, and headed back toward the grocery store parking lot. He couldn't screw this up. As much as he trusted Maggie, there was too much at stake.

Escondido and his army of drug runners were going down.

# CHAPTER EIGHT

M aggie loaded the supplies into her trunk, shaking her head at the growing pile of paper bags. Later, she'd transfer everything to the Jeep and head back to the cabins and stock them for the coming occupants. Right now, they stood empty, but she'd gotten word her guests would be arriving within the next two days, and everything had to be perfect. No mistakes, no missteps, no blunders.

*Guests.* What a misnomer. More like people who had nowhere else to turn. Who'd had all their options taken away, left with no resources to count on—except her. She both loved and hated she'd become embroiled in this subterfuge, but given the choice, she'd do it again in a heartbeat. After all, she could identify with them. Feel their struggles. Knew in excruciating detail the mental and physical anguish they endured, and the unimaginable choices that led them down a path from which there was no return. No way out.

Nobody could know. If anybody found out what was happening on her land, her property, she might be arrested. No, she *would* be arrested. She'd been threatened more than once, but she couldn't let the thought of going to jail keep her from doing what she had to—lives were at stake. What she did helped the ones who couldn't help themselves.

Closing her eyes, she leaned against the car, her hands atop the trunk, and felt the memories of that horrible night rush back, like it had happened yesterday. Fresh enough in her mind, she could almost feel her ex's forearm around her throat, squeezing tighter and tighter. Hear the blaring wah-wah of the police sirens. Smell the acrid stench of smoke from the teargas clogging her nose and choking her, making her gasp for air. She couldn't breathe. Heartbeat racing, adrenaline pouring through her body, she struggled against the crushing hold forcing her to her tiptoes as she tried to suck in air. Still felt the prick of the knife's blade beneath her breast.

"Maggie?"

She jerked free from the memories, staggering back a step away from Ridge. Breath soughed in and out of her lungs, and she sucked in a gulp of air, eyes wide. Now that she'd been pulled from her memories, she recognized the moment for what it was, because it had happened before.

*A panic attack.*

Wow, she hadn't suffered from one in such a long time, she'd thought—hoped—they were over. Yet here she stood, in the center of the grocery store parking lot, trembling with the aftereffects of falling head first into things better left alone. But the past once again reared its ugly head. She knew why. It was going to the tiny cabins, knowing they'd soon be filled, and she despaired over seeing anybody staying in them. Didn't matter, she'd made her choice. It was her decision. Right or wrong, she'd stand by her word—because there wasn't any other choice.

"What's wrong?" Ridge started to reach for her, and she took an unconscious step back. His hand froze at her movement, and he slowly pulled it back, lowering it to his side, his expression shuttered.

"Sorry. Nothing's wrong. I was lost in my thoughts, and didn't see or hear you."

"Maggie, you're white as a sheet and you're trembling. Did something happen?"

"No, Ridge, I swear everything's fine. Just a few unpleasant memories, nothing more. It's over. You ready to go?"

"Sure. Want me to drive?"

Maggie almost slumped with relief at his offer. The thought of climbing behind the wheel, with her hands shaking so badly she could barely hang onto the keys, scared her. Thank goodness Ridge came when he did, because she'd been close to succumbing to the panic attack. She'd be better soon, but coming down from the adrenaline high usually took time, and she didn't want Ridge to see her fall apart.

"That'd be great." She handed him the keys, hoping that he didn't notice her fingers quivering. Quickly walking around the car, she climbed onto the passenger seat, and fastened the seatbelt, crossing her arms over her chest.

*Just hold on. Once you're home, everything will be fine. You can do your meditation exercises. Focus on the positive. Concentrate on the here and now. The past can't hurt you. Never again. You're not vulnerable. You are strong. Capable. You are not a victim.*

Maggie focused on her breathing, slowing it down and taking controlled easy breaths in and out. She cut her eyes at Ridge, hoping he didn't notice her stiff posture, the rigid self-control she exerted to keep herself from falling to pieces.

"Unclench your muscles, Maggie. Uncurl your fists, stretch out your fingers, one at a time." His voice was soft, the tone soothing and reassuring. An unconscious hitch in her breathing had her closing her eyes, praying he wouldn't ask questions. It was too much, too soon, and she didn't have answers she wanted to share with him.

"That's it. Smooth, steady breaths. You're doing fine. We'll be home soon."

She didn't answer him, instead focusing on the road beyond the windshield, watching the white lines blend into each other with every mile. The rhythm of the tires on the asphalt hummed in the background like a lullaby, the soft shush-shush sound easing through her until her eyes drifted closed.

Ridge glanced over at the sleeping woman at his side. She'd finally relaxed enough to fall into a light doze, which gave him time to study her and wonder what had happened to trigger a panic attack. Definitely a PTSD reaction, he recognized it for what it was, because he'd seen several in the past. Whatever triggered it had to have been a doozy of a memory, because she'd be so pale, he'd wondered if she'd pass out.

He'd recognized the signs. The hyperventilating, the startle response when he'd called her name. Swaying on her feet, he'd reached for her, instantly wanting to comfort and ease her. Instead, he'd maintained the distance between them, at least physically.

With one hand on the wheel, he dug in his back pocket for his phone, and called Buckeye. Somebody fell down on the job when doing the assessment of Mary Margaret White, and he needed to fix that glitch before it became a bigger problem. Nothing in her background indicated anything traumatic in her past. In fact, her records were almost squeaky clean. Now, in hindsight, maybe they seemed a little too perfect.

"Hey, Ridge. How's it going in Texas Hill Country? Missing the big city yet?"

"Nothing wrong with loving Texas, my friend. You ought to try it sometime."

Buckeye laughed. "Thanks, but I'll stick to the sun and the sand. This Florida boy likes things a little more tropical. Cow patties and rattlesnakes aren't my idea of paradise, my brother."

"Don't knock it until you try it." Ridge stole another glance at Maggie, checking her breathing, and noticed the tiny sigh she gave before settling back against the seat. "Listen, I need you to do a little digging for me—off the record."

"Business or pleasure?" He could picture Buckeye sitting up straighter in his chair and cracking his knuckles over his keyboard, ready to explore the World Wide Web, coaxing it to reveal all its hidden secrets. There weren't many around who could finesse their way around the internet like Buckeye. There wouldn't be a byte of information on Maggie that he couldn't uncover. Ridge hated digging into her past, especially when it came to her personal life.

"Business," he started to reply, but then changed it to, "personal. I don't want anybody to know about me asking, or what you find. This is between you and me."

"No problem. Whose skeletons am I digging out of the closet?"

"Mary Margaret White, goes by Maggie. She owns a pretty sizable piece of property that straddles Burnet County and Shiloh Springs. DEA ran her, but my gut's telling me they missed something. It may be unimportant, but I get the feeling there's a whole lot more to Maggie White than what they found. I need everything. *Everything*."

"How soon do you need it?"

Ridge's hands clenched around the steering wheel, tightening until his knuckles were white.

"Yesterday."

Buckeye sighed, and Ridge could hear the clacking of keys as Buckeye began searching for info. "Gee, why am I not surprised by your answer? I'll get you something ASAP."

Ridge hesitated for a second, before he added, "Buckeye, somebody might have doctored her identity. Or made something important about her disappear. Nothing is adding up, and I don't like it." He kept his voice soft, not wanting Maggie to wake and hear him.

"Well, I'm guessing since the DEA did a background check, she's part of an ongoing investigation? Just asking, because I don't want to leave footprints in case somebody else starts digging into your gal."

"Definitely no footprints, buddy. E-mail me everything you find. And I owe you one."

"After you finish whatever you're working on, take a break. You haven't stopped working in I can't remember how long. Head on down to sunny Florida, and I'll treat you to beaches, babes, and all the beer you can drink."

"Deal. Thanks."

"No problem, catch ya later."

Disconnecting the call, Ridge turned the car into the drive leading up to Maggie's house, and pulled into the open bay in the garage. Maggie's eyes opened at the sound of the garage door closing.

"Welcome home, sleepyhead."

Her head whipped toward Ridge at the sound of his

voice. "What happened?"

"You had a little bit of a meltdown at the grocery, and I drove us home. No big deal." He jerked his thumb toward the trunk. "Gimme a minute and I'll unload your stuff. You want it in the kitchen?"

Maggie shook her head, opening the passenger door and climbing out. "No, that's okay. It's not for me; I picked it up for somebody else. There's nothing perishable in there, so it'll be fine until I drop it off. But thank you."

Ridge placed his hand on the small of her back, and she stiffened almost imperceptibly beneath his touch before relaxing and heading into the house. It might have been a leftover reaction from her panic attack earlier, but it still bothered him that her nerves seemed frayed. Whatever caused her meltdown, it must've been bad. Then again, posttraumatic stress sucked at the best of times. In his line of work, he'd seen far too much of it.

"Want something to drink?" Maggie swept into the kitchen and grabbed a couple of glasses from a cabinet. "I've got soda, water, or sweet tea."

"Tea, thanks."

While she fussed with the tea, Ridge heard the text alert ding on his cell phone. Pulling it free, he smiled at the message.

*Lunch at the Big House on Sunday. Unless you are bleeding or have lost an appendage, you WILL BE THERE. Love you.*

"Anything important?"

"My mother. Apparently, I'm being ordered home for lunch on Sunday. No excuses."

Maggie chuckled, setting the glass of tea in front of him. He slid onto the bar stool at the peninsula, laying his phone on the countertop.

"Sounds like your mother misses you."

"I saw her a week ago. I call her at least once a week when I'm on a job. With so many of us, my family tends to have large gatherings fairly often, especially if somebody has something to celebrate. The last few times I've been home, my brothers all got engaged. I swear, there's something in the water in Shiloh Springs, because they are dropping like flies. First Rafe, then Antonio. The latest is Brody. He's getting a ready-made family, because Beth has a daughter. Cute little girl, though she's been through a lot recently."

Maggie stood on the other side of the peninsula, and leaned against it, resting her chin on her hands. "It must be nice having a big family. Lots of brothers and sisters. I always wanted that, but I ended up an only child."

"Some days, I wished I was an only child. There were eleven of us, ten boys and one girl. Talk about crazy. That's not counting the ones who didn't stick around." At her perplexed expression, he explained. "We're all foster kids. I thought you knew. I guess I take it for granted that people know about my family, because everybody in Shiloh Springs does."

"You're all foster kids?"

"All except Nica. She's Momma and Dad's biological daughter. We tease her that she's the pampered princess, though it's not true. Our parents treat every one of us as their kids. It doesn't matter that we aren't blood kin, as far as they're concerned, that's the end of the story. We're theirs and they are our parents."

"I bet with all those children, there are some very interesting stories."

Ridge chuckled and toasted her with his tea. "You have no idea, Miss Maggie. Maybe I'll tell you a few someday."

She nodded toward his phone. "Shouldn't you answer you mother, let her know you'll be there?"

"Why don't you come with me?" He wasn't sure where the impulsive invitation came from, but it felt...right. Getting Maggie away from her home would give his team time to come onto the land and search for the road the smugglers were using. And he would love to see Maggie and his mother together. He'd bet they'd get on like a house afire. Ms. Patti would have every detail of Maggie's life story before the end of the day. She'd pry it from her, and Maggie wouldn't know what hit her until it was too late.

"Ridge, I don't think that's a good idea. You're here doing a job, and—"

"Maggie, when's the last time you did something spontaneous? From the little time I've spent with you, I've noticed you like order. Routine. Come on—take a break. Aren't you a little curious about meeting the infamous

Boudreaus of Shiloh Springs?"

"But it sounds like this is family time. They won't want a stranger horning in on their plans."

Ridge reached across and picked up Maggie's hand, squeezing it gently. "There's always room for one more around the Boudreau table. Be my guest, Miss Maggie. Please."

He realized he really wanted her to come with him. Wanted to show her where he came from, to introduce her to the people in his life that mattered. Give her a tiny glimpse into the real Ridge Boudreau, not the persona, the bits and pieces he'd played taking this job. He held his breath, waiting for her answer.

"If you're sure, then, yes, I'd like to come."

His pulse rate sped up, and he let out the breath he'd been holding. Grabbing his phone, he typed in a quick reply, telling his momma he'd be there, and he was bringing a guest, though he didn't mention his guest was a woman. There'd be a barrage of questions, a literal third-degree assault, and he didn't have time for that.

"Can't back out now, darlin'. Momma knows you're coming."

He had to prove Maggie wasn't involved with drug dealers. That she wasn't part of an international cartel smuggling drugs across Central Texas and distributing them through a pipeline that dispersed them across the United States. *He had to*.

Somehow in the last day, he'd realized the parameters of his job changed. He wasn't trying to simply find the people responsible for shipping poisonous junk into the U.S. and shutting them down. Proving Maggie wasn't part of the illegal drug trafficking had jumped to the top of his to-do list. Because he knew deep in his gut, she was innocent.

Proving it, though, might be harder than he thought.

# CHAPTER NINE

R idge waited until Maggie went to bed before sneaking out of the house, heading for the wooded area toward the west. A good portion of the area surrounding the house had been cleared back, resulting in an almost carpetlike blanket of grass sweeping outward, its appearance as soft as velvet. Jogging until he reached the trees, he moved further into the dense darkness enveloping the space surrounding him, letting his eyes adjust to his limited vision. He'd brought a flashlight with him, but wanted to be farther away from the house before using it, in case there might be prying eyes about.

Maggie had been slumbering peacefully when he'd left her office. Easing her bedroom door open, he'd studied her for far longer than he probably should have. Her hair spread across her pillow like a silken cloud, framing her beautiful face, and in sleep her expression softened, her lips plump and full. Dark lashes swept across her cheeks as she slumbered, and he watched as she shifted in her sleep, turning onto her side, and snuggling beneath the blanket. After her near meltdown earlier, he knew she needed the rest, and silently pulled the bedroom door closed, making his way outside through the kitchen.

A cursory check of the main rooms of the house yielded no clues. Although he knew it was fruitless, he'd checked over the room Maggie had put him in, as well as Henry's room. He needed to do a thorough search of her office, but she'd been in and out all evening while he'd worked on the security system. He knew he couldn't really dig deeper until she was out of the picture.

He had to admit, Maggie's property was stunning. Lush greenery dotted the landscape; even the untamed wildness had a beauty all its own. Switching on the flashlight, he maneuvered between the trees, appreciating the sprawling branches of the live oaks. Many of the gnarled, twisted branches reached upward toward the night sky, but occasionally he'd find himself climbing over the lower branches, closer to the ground. The flashlight illuminated the giant roots, a hazard he wanted to avoid. The last thing he intended was calling for a rescue from a sprained or broken ankle in the middle of nowhere.

The night was partly cloudy, though every once in a while, the moonlight drifted through the treetops, painting the forest floor with an eerie pale glow. Ridge searched for evidence of tire tracks, rutted pathways, anything to indicate trucks routinely traversed the area. His gut told him any easily traversed road wouldn't be this close to the house. But if he was a smuggler hauling a giant shipment of illegal cargo and wanted to throw off the Feds, he'd expect them to look as far from the house as possible, for fear of getting caught. Looking farther away from the civilized portion of the property made sense. Personally he'd do just the opposite. Knowing the Feds would look away from the inhabited areas, what better way to get away with hauling drugs than having the whole operation practically in Maggie's backyard?

The text alert chirped on his phone, and he pulled it out, scanning the message, before typing a quick response. The higher ups were getting impatient, and Daniel needed to give them an update ASAP. Wish he had better info to pass along—like Maggie being innocent—but he hadn't come up with anything to indict or clear her.

"What are you doing?" Ridge spun around at the sound of Maggie's voice, adrenaline rocketing through him until he was almost lightheaded. Where the heck had she come from, and how'd she find him so fast?

"Maggie?"

The look she shot him should have sent him up in a column of flames. Instead, he felt like a guilty five-year-old who'd been caught pinching a cookie out of the jar without permission. Her stare could have peeled paint at fifty yards. She crossed arms over her chest, her boot-clad foot tapping a staccato rhythm against the dirt and leaves.

"Answer the question, Mr. Boudreau. What do you think you're doing, slinking around my property in the dead of night?"

*Mr. Boudreau. Looks like I've managed to go from the big
house to the dog house. How am I gonna dig my way out of this
one?*

"I'm doing exactly what I've been hired to do, check out
the security on your land and make improvements. Finding
strengths and weaknesses, plugging holes where anybody
could get inside without setting off any alarms."

"At twelve thirty at night?"

"Are you questioning how I do my job, Maggie? I know
you checked my qualifications. What exactly did you expect,
that I'd sit behind the computer screen all day, give you a list
of upgrades and be on my way?"

"You could have told me you'd be going out. Instead, I
woke to an alarm blaring, and couldn't find you."

"Which alarm?"

"Huh?"

Ridge pinched the bridge of his nose between his thumb
and forefinger, and counted to three. Sometimes talking with
Maggie was worse than talking to a stone wall. The wall
might give him answers faster.

"Which alarm woke you?" Because he'd been careful to
turn off the ones where he'd planned on walking, and he
knew he hadn't tripped anything. If an alarm went off, that
meant—

"Come on." Grabbing her hand, he tugged her behind
him, moving swiftly through the trees, headed for the house.
If a sensor had been tripped, and Maggie was here with him,

that could only mean one thing. Someone else was on her property.

"Ridge, slow down."

"Maggie, if you heard an alarm, I didn't set it off. I need to find out where the sensor triggered, and find out what set it off. Could be an animal, but…"

"You don't think so." She picked up her speed, practically jogging to keep up with his long-legged stride. "When the computer alarm went off, I looked for you, figuring with all the work you've been doing on the system, there might've been a glitch. When I couldn't find you, I checked the security cameras and saw you heading this way. Since you hadn't bothered to tell me you were going out, I got…worried."

Ridge noted her hesitation before she tacked on the last word, and he'd bet she had a couple of others she considered using. Suspicious. Angry. Scared.

"I couldn't sleep, and decided to check out the wooded areas closest to the house. It was as spur of the moment decision, and I didn't want to wake you up."

"Next time, leave a note."

Ridge almost smiled at her ticked off tone. "Maybe I will."

Reaching the kitchen door, he held his finger to his lips. "Let me take a look around. Stay here."

"I don't think so."

"Maggie, please. Let me do my job. It'll only take a minute, unless I have to stand here arguing with you. I don't think anybody's inside, but I'd rather play it safe."

She huffed out an irritated growl, then leaned against the wall beside the door. "Fine. But if you're not back in two minutes, I'm coming in."

"Five."

"Three."

"Deal." He reached up and tucked a stray curl behind her ear, rubbing his knuckle against her cheek. "I'll be back."

Maggie watched Ridge silently make his way through the darkened kitchen, the only light the moonlight shining through the glass, stealing across the floor like a silent thief in the night. She absently nibbled on her thumbnail, a bad habit she'd thought she'd broken years ago. Guess she was a tad more stressed than she'd realized if she was falling back into old tics.

Everything outside seemed eerily quiet. Even the sounds of the insects had stilled, until all she heard was the waterfall splashing into the pool. She blew out a breath, ruffling the wispy bangs against her forehead, and counted in her head. If Ridge didn't show back up the second he'd promised, she was calling the police. *Or the company who monitors my security system.* When the alarm triggered, why in the heck didn't they contact her? That was their job, one she paid a ton of money for.

*Added peace of mind, my backside.*

When the kitchen light flared on, she nearly jumped out of her skin, until she spotted Ridge walking toward her. Flinging open the kitchen door, she raced inside, stopping mere inches from him.

"Well?"

"Coyote."

"A coyote? I don't—"

"It set of the motion detector by the front gate. Probably came across the road and onto your property. About three hundred yards from the front entrance, to be exact. Your security company had already contacted the police when they couldn't get hold of you. I gave them the all clear, but since the cops are already en route, we'll have to let 'em do their job."

Maggie swallowed down the lump in her throat, her mind racing a mile a minute. "We've had a lot of critters. Not surprising, since we're fairly rural, and there's a lot of land. But we haven't had any coyotes before."

"They're pretty common, although they tend to stay away from humans. We'll have to check, see if there's any scat around. Chances are good it's simply looking for food. If you don't leave anything around to attract them, they'll move on."

"Should I call somebody to come get it? Maybe animal control?"

Ridge reached forward and cupped his hand on her shoulder, squeezing gently. "You really don't have to worry. Coyotes aren't big on attacking humans. If you see it, you want to haze it. Most of the time, it'll run off."

"Haze it? What's that mean?" Maggie felt a stirring deep inside at the warmth of Ridge's hand, felt a tingling where his fingertips touched bare skin.

Ridge's smile made all sorts of interesting thoughts race through Maggie's head. And not a single one of them was PG rated. "Hazing means to make yourself the bigger alpha. Wave your arms, shout at them loudly. Make noise, be the aggressor. They'll run."

Without thinking, Maggie took a step toward Ridge. His deep brown eyes held a glint of humor and something else, burning with an intensity she felt like a physical caress.

"Uh-huh. Got it."

"Maggie, I—"

A loud buzz interrupted whatever Ridge had been about to say, and startled Maggie enough she took a step back, the sound finally making sense in her rattled brain. It was the front gate speaker. Placing a hand on her still quivering stomach, she took the few steps to the intercom and answered.

"Shiloh Springs Police Department, ma'am. We got a report from your security company that an alarm was triggered at this address."

Ridge walked over to stand beside her, and pressed the

button. "Dusty, is that you?"

"Yeah. Ridge? Or is this Shiloh?"

Shaking his head, Ridge answered, "It's Ridge. Come on up to the house, I'll buzz you in."

"Who's Shiloh?"

Ridge had started toward the door, and Maggie watched him pause, then glance back over his shoulder. "My brother. Twin brother."

"Twin brother," she whispered, eyes widening. "There are *two* of you? I can barely handle one."

"I heard that," he shot back, standing in the now open doorway. "And, before you ask, yes, we are identical twins."

"Is he as big a pain in the butt as you, cowboy?"

Laughter burst from Ridge's mouth. "Bigger. Ask anybody, I'm the good twin."

Maggie rolled her eyes. She wasn't buying it for a second. "I know you've got a huge family, but somehow the fact you had a twin somehow never made it into the conversation. Does he work in security, too?"

"In a roundabout way. He's a private investigator. A good one."

Maggie watched the headlights pull up and the car stop in front of her doorway. A tall, well-built man dressed in the de rigueur uniform that seemed a part of any Texas police officer's wardrobe walked to the front door. Ridge greeted him like an old friend.

"Sorry you got dragged out here on a wild good chase,

man."

"No big deal, Ridge. Wasn't all that busy anyway. Things are kinda slow around town right now. What happened?"

"Coyote. Wandered too close to a motion detector and set of the alarm. Maggie and I were outside, and didn't hear it. By the time we got back inside, the security company had already called you."

"And don't you love the way he talks for me?" Maggie walked up, and held her hand out to Dusty. "I'm Mary Margaret White. Maggie to my friends."

Dusty's smile lit up his face, and Maggie couldn't help noticing that he was a handsome man. From his dark blonde hair beneath his cowboy hat to the deep dimples carved into his cheeks, he was the typical small-town deputy you'd expect to read about in a romance novel. But standing next to Ridge, he didn't make her heart go pitter-patter. His good looks and spit-and-polish shine screamed All-American. Ridge, on the other hand, personified the bad boy with his dark hair reaching down past his shoulders, and mysterious brown eyes that seemed to darken with his moods.

*Why, oh, why do I always find myself gravitating toward the bad boy? Is it something in my genetic code that screams "tall, dark, and dangerous" is my drug of choice?*

"Pleasure to meet you, ma'am."

"Please, not ma'am. Call me Maggie."

"Thanks, Maggie. You've got a lovely place, but I'm

curious. Mind if I ask you a question?"

"Sure."

Dusty pulled off his cowboy hat, absently running a hand through his hair. "Why'd your security company call us—Shiloh Springs? Seems like your property's in Burnet County."

"Her land straddles both counties," Ridge answered before Maggie could open her mouth. "The cleared land and the house and surroundings are in Shiloh Springs. The unincorporated land, west of the house, is in Burnet County."

How'd Ridge know that? She hadn't mentioned it, and she was pretty sure Henry wouldn't have spit out that information. Something smelled fishy, and she watched Ridge. Took in his relaxed posture, his easygoing I'm-a-good-guy smile. Doubt niggled at the back of her mind that something seemed off, she couldn't put her finger on it. Not yet anyway.

"Gotcha. I'll fill out a report, get everything handled with the security company." Dusty shook Ridge's hand, and then Maggie's. "Y'all have a good night."

"Thanks, Dusty."

"No problem."

With that, he left, leaving Ridge and Maggie alone. Turning on her heel, Maggie headed back to the kitchen, yanked a pot out from under the stove, and slammed it atop the range. Then she pulled the container of milk from the fridge, pouring a generous amount into the pot and turning on the burner. Grabbing a cannister off the countertop, she dumped several heaping spoons of cocoa mix into the pot and stirred.

"Maggie?" Ridge stood across from her, watching her every movement.

"I know I'm not going back to sleep. I'm making some cocoa. Want some?"

"Okay."

Stomping across the kitchen, she reached into the dishwasher and pulled out two mugs, barely refraining from slamming them onto the counter, and leaned her hip against it, watching the pot on the stove. She was beginning to regret letting Ridge stay. Regret allowing him to work on her security. Shoot, she was beginning to think there was a whole lot more to Ridge's story than he'd told her—and not only did that tick her off, but it scared her. With everything coming to a head in a couple of days, she couldn't afford to make any mistake. One slip up and everything would fall apart, unravel like a loose thread. One good pull and it fell apart, destroying all she'd done, all the hard work and sacrifices. No, that couldn't happen.

Turning off the burner, she gave the chocolate a good stir and poured it into the waiting mugs, sliding one across to Ridge.

"Something's changed since we got home. Want to talk about it?"

Maggie studied him over the rim of her cup, taking a small sip of the hot chocolate, letting the warmth of the sweet drink sooth her. Even as a little girl, whenever she got upset, her mother had made her a cup of hot cocoa and promised that everything would be okay. It was her panacea to the outside world, the thing she'd go to when she was worried or upset. Tonight, for some reason, it wasn't working its regular magic.

"How did you know? About my land spreading over two counties? It's not really common knowledge—most people assume we're in Burnet County. But you didn't even hesitate. You knew."

"Maggie, I always do my homework when I start looking into a new project. I needed to know the details of exactly where your property lines begin and end. This isn't like setting up a series of wires and connections for a regular residence. We're talking thousands of acres of property, including your house. Regulations can vary from county to county. Heck, they can be different from city to city with regards to connecting with law enforcement and emergency services. It's not like the information is secret or anything. A couple of quick phone calls, and I had the details."

"Oh." She wanted to believe him, she really did.

"What are you thinking, Miss Maggie? I can practically see the wheels spinning around inside your pretty head."

"It's nothing. Just a long night. I think I'll turn in."

She lowered her head, not wanting to meet his gaze. For

some reason, Ridge seemed far too adept at reading her for someone she barely knew. She needed to stay on her toes, be ready, be vigilant. There was far too much riding on the next shipment for her to screw things up now because her libido decided it wanted to do the horizontal mambo with a stranger.

Picking up her mug, she cradled it in her hands, and turned to go.

"Good night, Maggie."

Without looking back, she answered. "G'night, Ridge. See you in the morning."

Instead of heading to bed, she kept walking, deep into the heart of her office. She had some digging to do, something she should have done the minute she'd caught him snooping around her property. She'd started before, but interruptions and getting the tiny houses ready kept her from following through.

It was time to find out exactly who Ridge Boudreau was, and what he was really doing on her land.

# CHAPTER TEN

Felicia arrived bright and early the next morning, with her usual level of exuberant excitement and overabundance of energy, making Maggie feel like a slug. Which seemed apropos, seeing she'd barely slept. Between the excitement of the night before, spending another couple of hours on the computer, and the enticingly erotic fantasies starring Ridge Boudreau keeping her awake, she felt like a sloth, moving through a pool of sticky tar. She stumbled into the kitchen and pointed at the coffee maker. Maybe an unintelligible grunt rolled from her lips, she couldn't be sure since she was brain dead.

Felicia grinned and poured her a cup. Wrapping her hands around the mug, Maggie inhaled deeply, letting the enticing scent of coffee fill her senses and slowly smiled. Herein lay her weakness, her kryptonite. If she had any plans to make it through her day as a fully functional human being, she needed an infusion of caffeine, although this morning, she'd probably need more than one. If she knew how, she'd mainline it straight into a vein.

"Good morning, sunshine. Late night?" Felicia grinned

and waggled her brows suggestively.

"Get a life, Felicia."

"But yours is so much more interesting. You look like you didn't get a lot of sleep. Was he that good?"

Maggie leaned forward and banged her head against the marble countertop. "Nothing happened. How many times do I have to tell you, Ridge is here for business only."

"Monkey business?" Felicia teased, pouring herself a cup of coffee. "The business of pleasure? Because looking at him, with all that I'm-a-bad-boy vibe coming off him, I'm betting he's a professional at pleasure."

"Ugh, do you ever think of anything besides s-e-x?"

"Sometimes. But teasing you is way too much fun." She took a deep drink of her coffee. "Really, Mags, you need a life." Felicia held up her hand when Maggie started to interrupt. "A real life, one outside your extracurricular activities. You have to let go of the past. Life isn't always ugly. There are times when it is downright beautiful. And you deserve that, Maggie. You deserve for the sun to shine on you and let you be happy."

Maggie knew her friend meant what she said, could hear the sincerity in her voice, but she was too jaded to believe in happily ever after. Felicia might still have blinders on and see the sunny side, but for Maggie, it was far too late. She'd settle for being content, because it sure beat the alternative.

"I need you to do me a favor." Maggie kept her voice low, almost at a whisper. "I've got some stuff in the trunk to restock the cabins. I was going to do it yesterday, but something happened, and I didn't get a chance. With Ridge here, I don't want to take a chance on him finding out. Can you make sure it gets there?"

"Of course. How soon do you need it? I can head over there now, if you want, and finish the cleaning when I get back."

"Anytime today will be fine. We've got a bit of time. I get antsy when I'm expecting…guests." Maggie took a big drink of her coffee, feeling the warmth spread through her like a hug. "It's mostly canned goods and a couple of things to help the time go by. Everything else looks great. I went by and cleared things out, made sure all the essentials were in place. Once the food situation is handled, we're all set."

"I get why you do this, Maggie, but have you thought about backing out just this once? With Henry not being here, you'll have to handle things on your own. Don't you remember what happened the last time? Maybe—"

"Felicia, I have to do this. No backing out and no cancelling. I made a promise. A commitment. No, even with Henry gone, things should be okay."

Felicia absently rubbed at an invisible spot on the counter, and Maggie wondered what the faraway look on her face meant. She didn't have to wait long to find out.

"What about asking Ridge to help? Wait, wait, hear me out," she implored when Maggie started to interrupt. "You know him better than I do, but Ridge seems like a good guy, who wouldn't hesitate to give you a helping hand. Just this once, Maggie, reach out and ask for help."

"I can't. If anything goes wrong, it's on me. I'm not dragging somebody else into this. It wouldn't be fair.

Felicia sighed. "Sometimes you're too darned stubborn for your own good. You're my best friend, and I worry about you. I know you want to save the world, but nobody said you had to do it singlehandedly."

"I have to do this. If I don't, who else will?" Maggie shook her head. "I'm not being a martyr, Felicia. I am fully cognizant that what I'm doing is against the law, and I will not drag anybody else along with me if I go down. But I can't stop. Not yet."

"Promise me you'll be careful."

Maggie reached across the counter and squeezed Felicia's hand. "I promise. Stop worrying, everything's going to be fine."

Felicia turned and walked across the living room, mumbling under her breath the whole way.

"I heard that," Maggie yelled after her.

"Good," she shot back, glancing over her shoulder. "But when they hold a funeral for your bullet-riddled corpse, I ain't coming."

"Sheesh, that's kinda morbid."

"I've got work to do. I'll take the stuff this afternoon." Felicia turned toward Maggie, standing by the sliding glass doors. "Be careful. I've got a funny feeling in my gut. That's all I'm saying, girlfriend. Be careful."

"Promise."

Maggie watched her friend glide out through the sliders, her expression guarded. She loved Felicia like a sister, even though she was a couple of years younger than her. Surprisingly, they'd met over ice cream. Maggie had been craving some and had driven into town. Felicia had been working at the ice cream parlor, and they'd hit it off instantly. Felicia was everything Maggie wasn't: outgoing, vivacious and had a zest for life unequaled by anybody she knew.

When she found out Felicia was working three jobs to pay for her schooling, Maggie had offered her the job of housekeeper, a few days a week at her place. She paid her an exorbitant amount of money, which enabled Felicia to only have to work part-time, and keep up with her class schedule. She'd graduate in a little less than six months with a degree and better job prospects than she'd imagined possible, and Maggie knew she'd probably head to Austin or maybe Dallas-Fort Worth after she got her degree. The thought of her friend moving away left her bereft. What would she do once Felicia was gone? Henry worked for her, at least for now, but eventually he'd move on, and she'd be truly alone.

*Get a grip, dummy. You've survived worse, and you'll get through this, too. Everybody leaves, it's a fact of life. Enjoy it while you can, because you know it'll all fall apart. But you survived. Life goes on, no matter how much you want to stop it, freeze time. Besides, if things go south, you'll have made your mark. Left a legacy to be proud of, even if nobody ever knows.*

Straightening, she walked into the kitchen and poured herself another cup of coffee, and headed to the office, intent of continuing her research into Ridge Boudreau.

Ridge met Delgado at the front gate of Maggie's property. Enrique Delgado had worked for Ridge's security company for a couple of years, and was good at his job. The official company was located in Austin, a little over an hour's drive from Shiloh Springs, which allowed Ridge to live in the town he loved, be close to his family, and yet still have a city presence for his business. His legitimate business, that is. His work with the DEA tended to take up more and more of his life these days, and he'd turned over a chuck of the day-to-day management to Delgado.

"I picked up the window and door sensors you asked for."

"Good. There are broken connections between several, so we're going to replace them all." Ridge leaned against the Texas limestone pillars that stretched upward on either side of the property's entrance, at least ten feet high. Arching across the top was an intricate scrollwork of metal and iron, twisted and molded into a design with the Lone Star emblazoned in the center. It was a striking feature, showcasing the drive up to the house, which was set back almost a half mile from the street.

An electronic double gate sat between the columns, with a keypad on the left one. Right now, the gates stood open, but they'd be firmly locked later against any uninvited guests, unless they scaled the fencing on either side of the limestone behemoths. Another security nightmare he'd be dealing with. Once the DEA's case was settled, he planned on making sure Maggie's home was nice and secure, his way of saying thank you for not only her hospitality, but her friendship and company.

"Ridge, do you want me to head up to the house now, or did you need something else?"

Ridge shook his head, pushing all thoughts of Maggie aside. Which was harder than he'd like to admit. He found himself thinking about her all the time. There was something about her that drew him in, fascinated him, made him want to uncover all her secrets and protect her from anything that might threaten her happiness.

"Wanted to ask your opinion. Take a look around, and tell me what you see."

Delgado stepped out of his car, and studied his surroundings carefully. Ridge did too, although he could see them every time he closed his eyes. The property entrance, the fence line, the paved road running in front of Maggie's house. The property across the street was unincorporated, overgrown with live oaks, mesquites, Indian hawthorn bushes, and Texas sage. It had to have been something special once, he mused, but it had been allowed to lie dormant, the brush growing with wild abandon until you couldn't see more than a foot or two before it became an entangled mess. A low barbed wire fence sat off-kilter, some of the posts having toppled and fallen from the weight of the branches, leaving a hauntingly beautiful visage.

"The fence along the front isn't going to be much of a deterrent to keeping anybody out. I spotted the pressure sensors every few feet, but that's definitely not enough. Heck, with a good enough running start, I could probably hurdle over it without touching the wood. I notice that further down there," he pointed, "there's taller fencing. I'd have to take a good look at it to tell you the security or lack thereof."

"Good catch. Let's head up to the house and get those sensors put in, and we can talk about what we can recommend to Miss White about upgrades."

Ridge slid onto the passenger seat and watched the gates close behind Delgado's car as they headed up the long, paved drive to the circular driveway in front of Maggie's house.

"Nice place."

"It is. Probably gonna be a lot of work, correcting the incompetence of whoever put in the existing system. The sensors you brought are just the beginning."

"Works for me." Delgado paused before asking, "Is this only a Sentinel Guardians job or something more?"

Ridge chuckled, not surprised that Delgado had picked

up on the situation. He was the only person at the company who knew about Ridge's job with the DEA, and he kept the company upright and above water whenever Ridge was out of pocket on a case. He was a good man to have around, and Ridge trusted him one hundred percent.

"Fixing up Maggie's security system is our secondary job. I'll introduce you, and you can get started with the sensor replacements and any rewiring. Then I'll fill you in on what I'm working on. But it's strictly between us. The homeowner doesn't know, and she's not going to. This will be over before she realizes anything else is going on. Got it?"

"No problem, boss. Let's knock out those sensors."

Opening the front door, Ridge headed for the computer room by Maggie's bedroom. That's where she'd been when he'd left earlier. He had a pretty good idea of what she was doing, and also knew that she wasn't going to find anything. There wasn't anything on the net about his governmental dealings. He was squeaky clean. All she'd find was what he'd told her, and it was the truth. He lived in Shiloh Springs. Parents were Douglas and Patricia Boudreau. He was a foster child in their home, had been since he was thirteen years old. Legally adopted by the Boudreaus, officially changed his name to Boudreau when he turned eighteen, and joined the Army. Served four years and came home to Shiloh Springs. Got an education in security expertise while in the service and put it to good use, apprenticing for the government for a year before opening his shop. Never married, no real long-term relationships. All true, except for the fact the DEA had recruited him right after he'd left the service, and he'd worked with them ever since. He had a knack for working undercover, blending in with the dealers, junkies, and the cartel leaders, helping to bring them down from the inside.

"Maggie," he called from the doorway, watching her intent concentration on something on the screen she was studying. Her startled gasp made him smile. "This is Enrique Delgado. He works for Sentinel Guardians Security, and he's going to be replacing the sensors on your windows. The ones we discussed, remember?"

"Of course I remember, I'm not senile." She stood and smiled at Delgado. "It's nice to meet you. Welcome to my home."

Ridge chuckled and tipped her chin up with his knuckle. "He gets a 'nice to meet you', and I got welcomed with a shotgun pointed at my face. Doesn't seem right, Miss Maggie."

"You introduced Mr. Delgado, and he was expected. You, on the other hand, trespassed on my land without asking. You're still lucky I didn't shoot your backside full of birdshot."

"Wait—you really held a gun on Ridge?" Delgado burst out laughing. Please tell me you have it on video somewhere. I would love to have a copy. Excellent blackmail material when I need a raise."

"I pay you too much already." Ridge glanced at Maggie,

saw her ready smile at Delgado's teasing. "Just wanted to let you know we're working, in case you heard noises and saw a stranger in your house. While he's working on the windows, I've got a few things I need to handle, but I'll be back in a couple of hours."

"Thanks for letting me know. Mr. Delgado, if you need anything, I'll be here, and my housekeeper, Felicia, is around, too."

"Yes, ma'am. Thanks."

"See you later, Maggie."

Ridge showed Delgado where to get started, and headed out to the garage. Maggie had given him permission to use any of her vehicles, and he'd spotted a nice ATV, which would get him where he needed to go a lot quicker than hoofing it. Grabbing the keys from the pegboard, he started it and drove away from the house, taking a well-worn path behind the garage. Might as well explore some of the property he hadn't looked at yet.

He hadn't made it far before his phone vibrated in his pocket. Slowing to a stop, he cut the engine, and pulled out his phone.

"Boudreau."

"Oh yeah? This is Boudreau, too." His father's deep voice held humor and affection, and Ridge soaked it up.

"Dad. Good to hear from you. What's up?"

"Your momma said you're coming for lunch tomorrow."

"Yes, sir. She orders, I obey."

"I see I taught you well." His father's chuckle warmed Ridge. The love he felt for the man was beyond explanation, and he thanked God daily that he'd been fortunate enough to have gained two people who'd made his life bearable after his mother's death. "I needed to check on you. You've been on my mind a lot lately."

Ridge pondered his father's words, wondering what was going on with him. "You saw me last week. Nothing's changed. I'm fine, I promise."

"Good. I've had this feeling, can't explain it. Like anticipation maybe. I know you're *working*," his father stressed the word, "so be careful. Something's in the air I can't put my finger on. I guess I needed to hear your voice."

"I'll see you tomorrow, Dad. I'm bringing a guest."

"Your mother told me. A girl?"

"Don't go getting any ideas. It's not like Rafe or Antonio or Brody. Maggie is simply a friend, and she's been under a lot of stress. I thought a dose of Boudreau family life would be just the thing to cheer her up."

"Good idea, son."

"Dad, tell Momma no matchmaking. I'm working for Maggie, and I don't need her or any of the other women trying to make more of it than it is. She's a nice person, but we aren't going to fall in love."

Douglas laughed at Ridge's protestation. "You keep telling yourself that, son. The harder you run, the harder you'll fall. I'll see you tomorrow."

"Bye, Dad."

Starting the ATV, Ridge headed deeper into the wooded area, intent on scoping out another section. Little by little, he was eliminating Maggie's land as the drug pipeline. Hopefully their intel was wrong, and the trucks wouldn't cross through her stretch of property. It had happened before. He really wanted to go to Daniel and tell him the DEA didn't have a case against Mary Margaret White. That she was innocent.

Because he had a gut feeling things were about to turn ugly, and he wouldn't be able to do a darned thing about it, except stand by and watch her be led away in handcuffs.

# CHAPTER ELEVEN

Sunday morning dawned with one of the most beautiful sunrises Maggie had ever seen. Taking her cup of coffee, she sat on the back patio and watched the sky come alive with color, painting the few low-lying clouds with all the majestic hues nature offered. She'd slept like a rock until right before dawn, and couldn't get back to sleep. So, she'd crawled out of bed and decided to take a few quiet moments for herself.

She loved this time of day, where everything seemed fresh and new. Reborn. A time for contemplating her past, her present, and her all-too-elusive future. Funny how she'd never envisioned having much of one. Not until Ridge steamrolled his way into her life, like an unstoppable freight train. Now, she wondered…if she'd done things differently, made other choices, chosen a different path, would she even be where she was today?

"Morning, Miss Maggie." Ridge stepped into her line of sight, a mug of coffee in his hand. His pants rode low on his hips, his bare chest was covered with a smattering of dark hair. She swallowed past the lump in her throat to respond.

"Good morning. Sleep well?"

"Yes." He nodded toward the still breaking sunrise. "Beautiful, isn't it?"

"Uh-huh. It's one of my favorite views from the house. Dawn breaking over the treetops, the water from the pool shimmering with color. And the quiet. It's like I'm such a tiny piece of the great big world around me, insignificant to the bigger picture."

Perching on the edge of her chaise lounge, he placed one hand on her knee, squeezing gently. "You'll never be insignificant. You're too full of life, Maggie. It's like you glow, radiate this internal...I don't know what to call it, maybe peace. Like you know who you are and what you want from life, and you'll move heaven and earth to accomplish it, and yet still remain the person you are deep within."

"That's beautiful, almost poetic." *And sounds nothing like me. Inside I'm a mess, with so many broken pieces, I'm afraid like Humpty-Dumpty, nobody will ever be able to put me back together again.*

"We've all got broken pieces," Ridge said softly, and Maggie blushed, realizing she'd spoken her thoughts aloud.

"Some more than others."

Ridge's eyes scanned her face, not in an unkind way. There was something in that look, a kindred spirit maybe, who understood all-too-well what it felt like to be broken. Curiosity crept into her thoughts, wondering what could have caused somebody as strong and upright as Ridge to shatter into a million tiny pieces.

"Want to talk about it?"

Did she? She'd hidden behind a façade of cavalier nonchalance for so long, kept everyone at arm's length for longer than she cared to think about. Yet there was something about Ridge that made her want to tell him. A gut instinct that said he wouldn't judge her and find her wanting.

"Did you know I was married before?" When he shook his head, she continued speaking softly because she didn't want to ruin this moment between them. "It was a long time ago. I married young, far too young to know what a mistake I made. I should probably tell you about my family, so you'll understand. My parents were great. The best parents anybody could ask for. I had a brother, Landon. He was a year and a half older than me. We didn't have a lot when we were growing up, not like you see here." She waved her hand around, indicating the patio, pool, and the house.

"Nothing wrong with not having money. It's how most of us lived."

"We had a house in an Austin suburb. A ranch-style house. Three bedrooms with a front porch and a postage stamp of a backyard. But it was home, and I loved it. My parents both worked. Dad drove a truck for a supermarket chain, and Mom worked for a pharmacy. One of those mom-and-pop shops like you'd see in the old TV shows, with sundries on the shelves, and a little soda fountain toward the back where they served milk shakes and ice cream."

Maggie stopped talking, her throat clogged with the memories of her mom, standing behind the counter, fixing shakes for her and Landon. He always got strawberry, and she got chocolate. She remembered her mother's smile, her gray eyes shining with hidden laughter when Landon would blow bubbles in his shake, making Maggie giggle uncontrollably. Every time she looked in the mirror, she saw her mother's eyes. The same gray color, the same shape, surrounded by dark lashes.

"My mom loved working at the pharmacy, futzing around behind the counter. She wasn't a pharmacist, so she didn't dispense drugs or anything, but everything else in the store she dealt with. On the weekends, when Dad was home, we'd make homemade ice cream. I won't go into details, but they came up with an ice cream treat that all the neighbor kids loved. Dad mentioned it to somebody at the grocery chain where he worked. Long story short, the chain could deal with manufacturing it and all the things that go along with selling it, so they put him in touch with a large company whose sole focus was ice cream novelties. They loved my parents' creation so much they bought it outright—lock, stock, and barrel—for a ton of money."

"That's amazing, Maggie. You must be very proud of them." Ridge's hand still rested on her knee, slowly massaging little circles on her skin, and Maggie closed her eyes against the feelings stirring deep within.

"I was." She felt the almost imperceptible acknowledgement at her use of the past tense, when the soft circles on her knee stopped for a mere second, before resuming. Before he could say anything, she plunged forward in her story. "All of a sudden, we had everything we ever dreamed. My parents built this house right away. We already owned this land. It had been in the family for generations, though nobody had done much with it. Not until we came into that ice cream money. Money changes everything, you know. Of course, both of them quit their jobs; they didn't need to work anymore. Landon and I were in high school, and it meant changing districts. Things were great for years. He graduated and went off to A&M. I followed two years later. Landon and I were coming home for fall break. My parents drove up to get us. It was pouring rain. We'd been on the road for almost an hour when a semi veered into our lane."

She stopped and took a deep breath. Even after all this time, thinking about the accident—what she could remember—wracked her with guilt. At the tightness in her chest, she closed her eyes, focusing on breathing. In slowly, out. Repeat.

"Maggie, darlin', I'm so sorry."

"Thank you. My parents…were killed instantly. Landon lingered in intensive care for almost twenty-four hours, though I never got to see him. They took me into surgery immediately, doing everything possible to keep me alive. You know what the hardest part was? All the people around me, telling me how lucky I was that I'd survived. I didn't feel lucky. I felt abandoned. I felt guilty because I survived and they didn't."

"I think it's perfectly normal to feel that. The loss you suffered wasn't only traumatic physically, but emotionally. Did you get help, counseling of some kind?" Ridge reached for her hand, and wrapped his around it, entwining their fingers.

"Yes, I did some one-on-one counseling with a psychiatrist at the beginning. Once I was allowed to leave the hospital, she suggested I attend a group for people dealing with loss. Grieving with others who've suffered is cathartic, at least that's what she told me. Anyway, I went. That's where I met Michael, my husband."

"You attended the same group therapy?"

"Uh-huh. Michael had lost his brother in a boating accident. They'd been out on Lake Travis and his brother fell overboard and drowned. So, we felt a bit like kindred spirits, working our way through loss. Maybe I was naïve, but all the attention he paid me made me feel special. Wanted. When Michael proposed, like a gullible fool, I leapt into marriage with both feet. We eloped to a Justice of the Peace and got hitched before I could realize what a colossal mistake I'd made."

"Sounds like he took advantage of your vulnerable state to push you into something you weren't ready for."

Maggie shook her head, and pulled her hand free from Ridge's, crossing her arms over her chest in a protective fashion. "Being young and foolish isn't an excuse. I went into the marriage with my eyes wide open. They might have been covered with rose-colored glasses, but I was stupidly, passionately, in love with Michael. He swore he felt the same about me. Just goes to show what a gullible fool I am."

"Never say that, Maggie. You were in shock from your loss, grieving, and it sounds like he manipulated you into something you were in no way ready for. Let me take a wild guess—he wanted your money."

"That's part of it, yes. But what he really wanted was a doll. Somebody who'd eagerly stay at home, cook his meals, wait on him hand and foot, and never say boo. And I did, because I wanted Michael to be happy."

"Why wouldn't he be happy? You are an amazing woman, Maggie. Any man would be blessed to have your love."

"That's…very sweet. I did love him, but it wasn't enough. Nothing I did was ever enough. I couldn't be the woman he wanted. I wasn't pretty enough. I wasn't thin enough. I wasn't meek or submissive. I guess once the shock subsided, my true personality, the real me, surfaced. Michael didn't like the real me, much less love me."

When Ridge sighed, she wanted to stop talking. She didn't want to tell him about the ugliness her marriage devolved into. Didn't want him seeing the side of her who'd allowed herself to be weak and ashamed. But once started, the words seemed to take on a mind of their own, spilling from her until she had to finish.

"The first time he hit me, I left. I walked away with nothing but the clothes on my back. I had money, lots of money, so I didn't end up in a shelter like most women less fortunate. I checked into a hotel and started making calls. Made sure Michael got taken off every account, every credit card. His name was removed from all the bank accounts. I cut him off at the knees, because I might have been a fool for marrying him, but I wasn't a doormat to allow him to get away with abusing me. No woman needs to allow anyone to hit them. That was and is a hard no for me."

"Good girl," Ridge murmured.

"Please, let me finish, so you know it all. If I stop now, I'll never be able to talk about this again." Getting off the chaise, Maggie took a few steps and stood at the edge of the pool, listening to the cascading water from the waterfall splashing against the rocks, the sound a soothing backdrop to her frazzled thoughts.

"I had to get a restraining order, have my lawyer remove Michael from the property physically, and believe me, that wasn't a happy, fun time. He used the legal system like a pro, trying to stay in this house. We already had a security system my dad installed when they built the house, and I got it upgraded. That's where Henry Duvall comes into the picture. He came highly recommended by several prominent people. The guy knows his stuff when it comes to electronics and surveillance. Anyway, Michael wasn't allowed anywhere near me. And before you ask, yes, I filed for divorce. Michael wasn't having any part of agreeing to a divorce, no matter how big a settlement check I offered, and it was a lot. I wanted him gone, out of my life for good, and was willing to pay to make it happen."

"I'm so proud of you," he whispered in her ear. Lost in her memories, she hadn't heard him move to stand behind her. When his arms slid around her waist, she leaned against him, indulging in the feeling of warmth and safety offered with his silent support.

"I was home alone when Michael showed up. Henry had gone to town to get something, I can't even remember now what it was. Felicia only came in the mornings, and she'd already left. He—Michael—rammed his Hummer through the front gates, pushing them aside like they were tin cans. He pounded on the door, demanding I let him in. The sound of his shouting, there was something different about it this time. Not that he didn't lose his temper and yell; he did. A lot. But this time, I don't know, it sounded like he didn't care anymore. He wasn't going to get back into his car and leave. I could feel it in my gut. I went for my shotgun. I wasn't going to be defenseless if he somehow got through the doors. You've seen my front doors; they aren't easy to get through with anything less than a battering ram."

"They aren't, but I've got a pretty good idea of what he did. I noticed the repair work in the limestone around the entranceway. Meant to ask you about it. He drove his Hummer through the front doors." The way he said it wasn't a question, but she answered him anyway.

"Yes. By the time I realized what he was doing, it was almost too late. The doors were no match for a six-thousand-pound Hummer. I ran for the back doors, intent on getting away. He…he was on me before I'd made it halfway. Tackled me from behind, and when I landed on my stomach, the shotgun flew from my hands." Maggie trembled, remembering how helpless she'd felt sprawled on the living room floor, Michael's weight pressing against her, smothering her, leaving her gasping for breath.

"We struggled. It was pretty one-sided, because Michael was a large man, over six feet tall, and he worked out. He backhanded me across the face. I remember thinking at the time it didn't hurt. I guess I'd gone numb, locking everything away. I do remember thinking if I didn't provoke him, didn't respond to his tirade or his fists, he'd stop."

"Did he—stop?"

Maggie's head jerked in a brief nod. "The alarm triggered the minute he hit the front doors with the Hummer. When I didn't respond to the security services' call, they must've notified the police. I heard the sirens, knew help was coming, and I must have made a sound, or moved the wrong way, because Michael grabbed me by my hair and dragged me to the kitchen. Then he grabbed a butcher knife—to this day I don't know why he didn't go for the shotgun. The local police got here first, flashing lights and sirens blaring. The county sheriff showed up next. I can't remember if it was Shiloh Springs or Burnet County."

"Shh, it doesn't matter. Finish it, Maggie. Get it all out, and then we'll let it go."

"I wish I could let it go. If only it was that easy."

Ridge's arms tightened around her, and she leaned her head against his shoulder. How long had it been since she'd allowed anyone to hold her? Touch her? Standing here with Ridge's arms around her, it felt like she was coming alive. For the first time since she'd gotten out of the hospital, after the accident and losing her family, she felt like a tiny blossom opening to the sunlight. And it scared her, because Ridge was temporary. Once the job was done, he'd move on, without a backward glance. She couldn't afford to risk her heart. Look what happened the one time she'd risked it. No, allowing Ridge close would require her trusting him, and no matter how good or kind or upstanding he seemed, she didn't trust him. Not completely. And she never would.

"Michael put the knife to my throat when the police came through the door. I remember everything seemed to slow, like an old movie clip. Heard the officers telling him to drop the knife and let me go. Him holding the knife close to my throat. I can still remember the coldness of the blade against my skin. It's funny how some things have faded with the passage of time, and yet others are crystal clear, as if it happened moments ago. Everyone was still, all these guns pointed toward me—well, they were pointed toward Michael, but he held me in front of him, the perfect human shield."

"Maggie—"

"One of the officers tried to reason with him, promised nobody would get hurt if he released me. Michael refused, demanding they let him go, and hitching the knife higher against my throat. It was a standoff, one nobody could win. Someone needed to do something, and the police couldn't take the shot. It wasn't like you see in the movies, where the SWAT team has a sniper ready to take out the bad guy with the perfect kill shot. These were simply men and women trying to deal with a situation they don't normally see and honestly weren't ready to face. I'll admit I was terrified, because Michael wasn't right in the head. I think he wanted the cops to shoot him."

Ridge sighed. "Suicide by cop. He probably thought it would make him some kind of martyr." His lips brushed against her cheek, so soft and gentle she thought she might have imagined it. "Did it work?"

She drew in a shaky breath. "No. I did something foolish, although at the time I thought I was doing the exact right thing. I—went limp. Let everything go and forced Michael to struggle to hold me up. The knife…slipped…and went into the side of my neck." Maggie ran her fingertips across the scar on her collarbone, recalling the jolting pain as the blade cut deep.

Ridge let loose a string of curses, and the corners of Maggie's lips lifted in a smile. The entire time she'd know him, she'd never heard him use any colorful language. Now, he was making up for lost time, coming up with some inventive ones she'd never heard before.

"When I tumbled forward, the police rushed forward and subdued Michael, wrestling him to the floor and handcuffing him. They hauled him off to jail within minutes."

"Good. He's in prison, right?"

"I wish it was that simple. The police discovered his parents' bodies later that same day. Turns out Michael had killed them both before coming after me. He never intended to let me live. He left a note at his parents' home, admitting to killing them and to killing his brother years prior. Said he hadn't drowned all those years ago, Michael had pushed him out of the boat. The letter stated he wouldn't let me leave him, because I belonged to him. After he was arrested, he killed himself in his cell."

"Aw, sweetheart, I'm so sorry."

Ridge turned her gently in his arms, his hold loose, giving her the freedom to step away if she wanted. Instead, she did the opposite. She twined her arms around him and stepped closer, allowing herself to finally release the pent-up tension she'd been holding while she told Ridge her story. *Her history.* She'd laid herself bare, exposed like a nerve ending, raw and bleeding. What he did with the knowledge she shared was up to him, but in telling him about her past, unburdening herself, she felt lighter, freer.

"You are an amazing woman, Mary Margaret White. I am so very proud of you."

Her eyes widened at his words, his praise a balm to her battered spirit. When his hand cupped her cheek, she closed her eyes, leaning into his touch. The feel of his lips on hers sent a frisson of electricity spinning through her, and she responded, returning his kiss. Tangling her fingers in his hair, she tilted her head, deepening their kiss. Something about the touch of his lips against hers, she wanted it to go on forever. Nothing else mattered except the feel of Ridge's lips on hers, the bubbles of excitement swirling through her body at this simple yet explosive touch. There was a magic in this kiss, it was more than special—it was life-altering—and she wanted to be swept away on this swirling sea of emotion that was Ridge Boudreau.

Reluctantly pulling back, she ran a fingertip against his parted lips, feeling the silky softness of his mouth beneath her touch. Every instinct inside her screamed to pull Ridge close, feel his intoxicating kiss again, be swept away beneath the whirlpool of emotions roiling inside her. She felt giddy, like a teenager with her first crush, instead of a woman who'd seen too much in her lifetime to trust the feelings aching for release.

She pulled back and gave him an indulgent smile. Ridge's eyes searched her face for a long while, before he finally took a step back, and grasped her hand, bringing it up and brushing a tender kiss across her knuckles.

"Thank you for sharing with me, Miss Maggie." He brushed his thumb across her lips, his dark eyes brimming with emotion, and she almost gave in to temptation and kissed him again. Instead, she took one step back and then another.

"I'm not whole, Ridge. I may never be again. I've put the pieces back together as best I can, but some days I'm afraid the glue won't hold, and I'll be little more than a stack of jagged edges that I can't reassemble into anything resembling normal."

"Don't sell yourself short, sweetheart. You are one of the most grounded and stable people I've ever met. I know what a broken person looks like. Sounds like. I was in the Army. Trust me, there are broken people who find a way to keep going, and some who never make it all the way back. *You* made it back, and because you were broken, you mended all the pieces, and they are stronger than before. You *will not* break."

She felt the tears welling in her eyes, and barely kept them from overflowing. "Thank you." She sniffed back the tears, and gave him a watery smile. "Want some breakfast?"

"Only if I get to help."

"You're on."

On the way to the kitchen, she stopped. "Ridge, about lunch—"

"Nope, you're not getting out of it that easy. Besides, Momma knows you're coming, and trust me, you do not want to disappoint Patricia Boudreau." His accompanying grin made her chuckle.

"Got it. No disappointing your mother. Now, let's eat. I'm starving."

# CHAPTER TWELVE

From the corner of his eye, Ridge watched as Maggie got her first good look at the Boudreau home or, as it was known throughout Shiloh Springs, the Big House. It had gotten the nickname from the foster boys, who'd grown up calling it that. In the beginning, they'd looked on it as a prison from which they couldn't escape. The name stuck. But it was also a large-sized house with enough property to make it the biggest spread in the county. It had to be to hold all the rambunctiousness of a passel of adolescent males, intent on mischief. He wondered if she'd compare it with her home, and find it lacking. The structures were as different as night and day, each unique in its own way, but he admitted to being partial to the Big House—because it was home.

"Oh, wow," Maggie breathed out the words, "it's beautiful."

The tension Ridge felt melted away at her simple compliment, and gave the aging beauty the once over, trying to see it from a dispassionate eye. Even having lived here for years, he still got a knot in his stomach on coming to the Big

House, because it was *home*. Two stories high, it reminded him of an old antebellum plantation house, the ones he'd seen when he visited family in New Orleans. Painted white with dark green shutters on the windows, it gave the house its stately appearance. There were rounded columns on both the first and second floors, with porches wrapping around both levels. A brick pathway led to the front porch and the door had a rounded arch above.

To the side, an addition had been built years ago, and blended seamlessly with the original structure. Not surprising, since his father owned a construction company. He remembered his momma mentioning she wanted to add on a master suite and within days, construction had commenced. Ridge smiled at the memory. That was all it took. If Momma wanted something, Dad moved heaven and earth to make it happen. The love his parents shared was priceless, and he couldn't help but wonder if he'd ever find anything close to it for himself. Glancing at Maggie again, the thought sprang into his head maybe he already had.

He pulled up in front of the house, parking with all the other cars. It looked like a good chunk of his family was already here. The more the merrier.

"Welcome to my home, Maggie."

"Thanks. Are you sure I look okay?"

"You look beautiful. Don't worry, these things aren't formal. It's just lunch with the family."

She gave an inelegant snort. "For you, it's lunch with the

family. For me, I'm meeting your parents. Oh, wow. I'm meeting your parents!" Her voice rose with each syllable, and Ridge found himself chuckling.

"Breathe, Maggie. I promise they don't bite. They are going to love you. Especially my momma. I can't promise she won't ask you questions though."

"This still feels weird. I mean, you're working for me. We hardly know each other." Her fingers twined together in her lap, twisting over and over, until he finally laid his hand over them.

"Everything is going to be fine. And you're practically a neighbor, since half of your property is in Shiloh Springs."

"County. Shiloh Springs County. I can probably count on one hand the number of times I've actually been in your town."

Leaning forward, he brushed a quick kiss against her cheek. "We'll have to change that."

Climbing out of the car, he walked around and opened Maggie's door. He'd borrowed her sedan since he wanted her to feel comfortable, and having something that belonged solely to her would give her an illusion of control.

"Come on, Ridge. Hurry up or you're gonna miss it." Nica stood on the edge of the porch, a silly grin plastered on her lips. Her long blonde hair caught the sun haloed around her face, and he was struck again by how much she'd grown up. It felt like she went from a kid in pigtails to a young woman going to college in the blink of an eye.

KATHY IVAN

"What's going on?"

"It's a surprise, but you better hurry." Nica straightened when she caught sight of Maggie at his side, and if it was possible, her smile got even bigger. "Who's your friend?"

Finishing the walk up to the steps of the front porch, he lightly grasped Maggie's elbow and escorted her the rest of the way. "Maggie, this is my baby sister, Veronica."

"Seriously? That's how you're going to introduce me?" Rolling her eyes, she pushed Ridge aside and held out her hand. "I'm Nica. Nobody calls me Veronica." She jerked her thumb toward Ridge. "Except this dope when he's trying to annoy me."

"Maggie White. I totally understand. I'm Mary Margaret, but I prefer Maggie."

"Cool." Nica hip-checked Ridge aside and looped her elbow through Maggie's and shot a triumphant glare toward Ridge. "Now, can we go inside?"

"Lead the way, Sis."

He followed behind, watching Nica animatedly chatting with Maggie, and saw Maggie smile at something she said. The words weren't important. He wasn't paying attention to them anyway. He loved the open, giving welcome his baby sister gave Maggie, helping her to instantly feel a part of things. Chalk one up for Nica, who'd somehow figured out Maggie was nervous and immediately jumped into action. Actually, it was almost like seeing a miniature version of his momma, and he could understand anew why his dad fell in

114

love with her.

Nica led Maggie through the house and out to the patio, where Douglas stood manning the enormous barbecue grill. The scent of wood smoke and BBQ sauce wafted toward him, and Ridge felt his stomach rumble. He was ready for some of his daddy's famous ribs, and maybe a burger or two. Nica had put on a full head of steam, practically dragging Maggie across the patio toward his momma, who sat on one of the padded chairs grouped around the side, along with a matching love seat and a few other chairs, already filled with the other women. He spotted Tessa and Beth, with Jamie sitting between her feet, a coloring book in her lap, furiously scribbling at the pages. Jill Monroe sat next to Tessa. He hadn't seen her in a while, but the good news was, if she was here that meant she'd brought one of her cakes.

He walked faster, but didn't quite catch up before Nica hauled Maggie to stand in front of his mother. Turning her head, she gave him a wink over her shoulder.

"Hey, Momma, look who I found. This is Mary Margaret, but she likes to be called Maggie." She kept her arm looped through Maggie's, as if afraid she'd bolt the second Nica turned her loose. When she whipped her head around looking for him, he almost laughed at her wild-eyed expression. Guess he'd better rescue her.

"Afternoon, Momma." Leaning down, he pressed a kiss against his mother's cheek before straightening and walking toward Maggie and his sister. Looping his arm around his sister's neck, he pulled her close and tousled her hair as she struggled to get free. Pulling her close, he whispered in her ear, "Thanks, Nica."

"You're welcome." When he let her go, she started around him and then jumped on his back, wrapping her arms around his neck and her legs around his waist, plastering herself against him. "By the way, I like her." With that, she jumped off, backpedaling quickly, laughing.

Facing his mother, he saw her indulgent smile. Nica was special, their miracle girl. Everybody loved her; all her foster brothers adored her. They might call her the pampered princess and claim she was spoiled, but nothing could be farther from the truth. She pitched in as much as any man on the ranch when she was home from school, and even before. Growing up with almost a dozen big brothers, she'd been a tomboy and daredevil most of her life. There was a zest for life inside Nica, and he prayed nobody and nothing quelled her spirit, or they'd answer to him and a whole bunch of pissed off big brothers.

"Maggie, why don't you come sit by me? Ridge, pull that chair over here, please."

"Thank you, Mrs. Boudreau."

"Ms. Patti!" Multiple voices chimed in at the same time, followed by laughter.

"That's right, call me Ms. Patti." His mother smiled, her eyes twinkling. "Son, why don't you go help your daddy with the grill? I know he's looking forward to talking with you."

Ridge knew a dismissal when he heard one, though he loathed leaving Maggie undefended. Not that he was afraid she couldn't hold her own, but the odds were a little unbalanced. Four against one seemed a little one-sided. His gaze met Maggie's and he searched for any sign of nervousness or anxiety, and was surprised when he saw her smile. It lit up her face, and the sight filled him with a surge of happiness.

"Go ahead, I'll be fine."

"Okay. Wave if you need me, I'll be right over there." He pointed toward his father, who raised his tongs and nodded.

"Son, it'll be fine. The ladies will have a chat, and then it'll be time for lunch."

He turned and started toward the grill, but spun around. "When we got here, Nica was all excited about some surprise, and rushed us back here. What's going on?"

His momma's enigmatic smile was all the answer he got. Guess he'd find out later.

The rock in the pit of Maggie's stomach let her know it was interrogation time. Oh, she was sure the women wouldn't rake her over the coals. Didn't seem to be their style. But they'd get answers to whatever questions they deemed important. *Might as well get comfortable.*

"Here you go." Nica's hand came from behind, handing her a can of Dr Pepper. "I hope this is okay. If you want something else, I can grab it."

"This is perfect," Maggie took the offered can and popped the tab. "Thanks."

"No problem." Coming from behind her, Nica dropped to the ground at Maggie's feet, and opened her own soda. "You ready for this? I've got the bright lights and rubber hoses ready, but something tells me we won't need 'em, am I right?" Her grin was infectious and Maggie found herself smiling.

"Keep them handy just in case, but I'll try and answer your questions."

"Nica, I told you we aren't going to give Maggie the third degree. This is a friendly lunch. I expect you to behave."

"Momma, Maggie's a Southern girl. She knows what it means when you're invited to a family dinner. Right?" Nica looked imploringly at Maggie, as if pleading with her to not get her in trouble.

"It's fine, Mrs. Boudreau…I mean, Ms. Patti. I don't have any secrets." The second words left her lips, she wanted to yank them back, because she did have secrets. Secrets that could get these ladies in trouble if they discovered them. She'd have to watch every word from here on out, because there was something about Ms. Patti and Nica that made her feel relaxed and comfortable. Maybe a bit too comfortable because oddly, she found herself wanting—needing—their approval. Which was ridiculous. There wasn't any reason their opinion about her mattered one way or another.

"Maggie, let me at least introduce you to the others. This is Tessa Maxwell, she's engaged to my son, Rafe. Then, next to her is her sister, Beth Stewart, who's engaged to my son, Brody. The young lady sitting across from you is Jillian Monroe."

"Which son is she engaged to?" Maggie asked and watched a splash of color sweep across Jillian's cheeks.

"None of them," Jillian responded.

Maggie heard Ms. Patti's murmured, "not yet", followed by Nica's snicker, and knew there was a story there.

Ms. Patti pointed at Nica. "And you've met our youngest."

Nica raised her soda in salute before taking a drink.

"We are waiting for a couple more arrivals before we eat. Antonio and Serena are driving in from Austin. They spent a couple of days there, but they're coming home. Should be here soon. Liam's at a job site, dealing with some issue that came up, but he's going to try and make it." She looked over her shoulder toward the grill. "The menfolk are with my husband, Douglas. There's Rafe, Brody, Chance, and, of course, Ridge.

"Where's Heath?" Beth looked up from studying her

daughter's picture to ask Ms. Patti. "I thought he'd be here for sure."

"He left early this morning. Something came up with his job, and he had to get back." A melancholy look graced her face, and Maggie knew she was thinking about her son, Heath. She assumed Heath must be another Boudreau.

"I'm worried about him."

"I am too, Beth. I find myself hoping every day he'll call and say he's moving back. It's so hard knowing he's halfway across the country, working a dangerous job. I know I'm a mother hen, but I want all my boys around me close, so I know they're safe."

"It'll be okay, Momma." Nica rolled to her knees and hugged her mother. "Heath's smart and he's good at what he does. Plus, he's careful. He'll be alright."

"I know that here," Ms. Patti pointed to her head. "But, it's hard to convince myself here." She pointed to her heart. "I'm a mother. It's my job to worry." Shaking her head, she plastered on a smile. "Maggie, tell me about you. How'd you and Ridge meet?"

Maggie pondered for a second or two, trying to decide whether to give a nice generic version or to tell the truth. The truth won.

"The first time I met Ridge, I held a gun to his head."

# CHAPTER THIRTEEN

The afternoon barbecue had been a rousing success. Everybody seemed to adore Maggie, especially the ladies of the family. Somehow, they'd bonded, if the shouts of laughter coming from their circle earlier was any indication. When they'd gathered for food, his momma had squeezed his arm, and said she liked Maggie. High praise indeed. But he was still waiting for the other shoe to drop, as they say. The big surprise Nica had hinted about earlier when they'd arrived.

The food had been eaten, and dessert consumed. When Jill had brought out the cake she'd made, the family had descended on it like a rampaging horde, barely taking time to come up for air. It had been a thing of beauty, or at least it had looked pretty, until his brothers glommed onto it like they'd never seen cake before.

Now, with soft music playing in the kitchen, the chairs had been pushed back onto the grass, and the area cleared. Rafe and Tessa swayed to the music, and Brody and Beth danced with Jamie held in their arms, her soft giggles the sweetest sound. He loved hearing her laughter, because it hadn't been all that long ago, she'd been kidnapped by her own father, in his deluded plan to extort money for her return. But she'd been rescued and didn't seem any worse from having gone through the ordeal. The family still kept a close eye on her, never leaving her alone for a second, even though her father was no longer a threat. He was locked away in solitary at Huntsville, where he couldn't hurt her or Beth again.

Maggie sat with his mother, softly talking, which gave him time to watch her without her knowledge. She was a beautiful woman, inside and out. More so since she'd revealed what her life had been like with her ex-husband. He couldn't believe the bravery she'd shown, or the devastating losses she'd suffered. Yet she'd risen above it all to become a strong, resilient woman, one he admired.

"I like your Maggie." His father leaned against the pergola's support, and watched his wife with Maggie, an indulgent smile crossing his lips.

"I wouldn't call her my Maggie. We barely know one another."

"Doesn't matter how long you've known someone. There's a...sweetness about her that's inherent to her personality. She reminds me of your mother." He stopped for a second, before adding, "Your biological mother."

Ridge started at his father's words. Although he thought about his biological mother all the time, she'd been gone long enough that the aching loss didn't hurt when he did.

She'd fought a long and hard battle, but when she'd known there wasn't going to be a miracle cure and the pain from the cancer got to the point where she couldn't deal with it, she'd turned to her best friend, Patricia Boudreau, to raise her sons after she was gone.

"I hadn't really thought about it, but you're right. She does kind of remind me of her."

"Course, she's got a bit of my Patti's gumption, too. Heard her tell them she pulled a gun on you." Douglas quirked his head, indicating he wanted to hear a little more about that story.

Ridge chuckled. "She did. First time we met. I went out to her place to do some consulting work on her security. Unfortunately, she didn't know I was coming. Figured I was an intruder. She happened to have her shotgun with her, and kindly asked me to get off her land."

Douglas started laughing, and it grew until he was bent over and nearly out of breath. When he finally straightened, Ridge watched him rub a teardrop from the corner of his eye. "Remind me to tell you about the time Ms. Patti pulled a gun on me. No, not now, we ain't got time." He nodded toward the doorway, where Chance and Dane stood. "Got a couple of announcements to make. We'll talk later."

Walking to the center of the patio, Douglas motion for Ms. Patti, who joined him. "We've got a couple of announcements to make today, which is why we're here. First, Brody and Beth, y'all want to go first?"

Ridge had a pretty good idea of what was coming, and felt a well of happiness for his brother.

"Pretty sure this isn't going to be a surprise to anybody, but Beth said yes. So, we're getting married!"

"Congratulations!" Rafe slapped Brody on the back, grinning from ear to ear. "Not that I'm surprised, you all but proposed to her already."

"I know, but there's more. We've set a date."

Shouts and squeals of excitement overrode most of the rest of what he was saying. Ridge grinned too, because he'd seen how much Brody loved Beth, and knew he would move heaven and earth for her if he could. It hadn't been all that long ago his brother had been moody and moping around because he was afraid to go after the woman he loved, and look at him now. A fiancée and a ready-made family rolled into one.

"When?" Nica's voice drowned out everyone else's. "You said you set a date, so when is the Big Day?"

Brody looked at Beth and smiled. "Christmas Eve."

"But that's not enough time. Weddings take months and months to plan, to get everything right. You need—"

"Nica, I have everything I could ever need or want right here." Brody squeezed Beth's hand, and hoisted Jamie higher on his shoulder. "We don't want anything fancy. A small ceremony with our family and a few friends, and we'll be happy."

"It sounds perfect," Beth smiled sweetly.

Ridge half-listened as the rest of the family gave the couple their well wishes and talked wedding plans, and he noticed Maggie had moved a little farther away from the crowd, shoulders stiff. She'd turned away and stared into the distance, and he knew hearing talk of weddings and happily ever afters probably upset her, especially after she'd revealed the disaster her own marriage devolved into.

He started toward her, but felt a hand on his arm, and looked down to see his momma standing at his side. "Why don't you take her to the gazebo, Ridge? This is all a bit overwhelming, especially since she doesn't know us all that well yet. Give her a bit of a respite. Your daddy's announcement can wait. I'll fill you in later, promise."

"Thanks, Momma." Bending down, Ridge brushed a kiss against her cheek, and walked over to Maggie.

"Want to take a walk with me? There's something I'd like to show you."

Her eyes widened a bit and she nibbled her bottom lip before nodding. "Sure."

Without a word, he took her hand in his, giving it a little squeeze, and then held it tight as he led her across the grass behind the house and around the side, past the master suite patio, flanked by glass doors. Over the past few years, this side porch became his mother's morning retreat. It was a comfortable, charming vignette, showcasing a set of chairs and a glass table. The intimate space provided privacy and an innate sense of romance and solitude. This master suite was his mother's sanctuary away from screaming kids and cantankerous teens. Now it was her oasis of calm from the real estate business, and a getaway from the day-to-day life on a working ranch.

Maggie studied everything as they passed. He heard her intake of breath at the decorative urns and pots overflowing with deep green ferns and flowers, their strikingly vivid colors evidence of somebody's green thumb. Not his, though. He had what he always called the black thumbs of death. Couldn't keep a plant alive, no matter how hard he tried. Continuing around the corner, he walked farther along the grassy surface until he came to a bank of trees.

Finally, he stopped when they reached their destination. A white-roofed gazebo sat in the center of a clearing, surrounded by a stand of tall trees. White lattice around the bottom, a circular roof perched on top of the structure, and the sides were open. The base of the gazebo was surrounded by tall ornamental grasses swaying gently in the soft breeze. Pink and white roses climbed along the structure, edging close to the roof, and wrapping around the columns. The sweet scent of the flowers wafted in the air, perfuming the area around them.

At the center of the enchanted structure stood the high-light of the magical scene—a well. The smooth stone and wooden structure should have looked incongruous in such a fantasy setting, but it didn't. Inside the well, a rope was attached to a wooden arm and handle, a bucket swinging from the end of rope. His mother called it her wishing well. As a young boy, he'd tossed coin after coin into its depths, wishing for the impossible.

A white-painted bench sat partially hidden within the walls of the gazebo. Tiny white lights ringed the bases of the trees, as well as along the inside of the roofline. Ridge flicked a switch inside the entrance, and smiled as the lights turned on, a soft golden glow within the magical structure. His father had added them a few years back during the holidays, and they decided to leave them up year-round.

"This is amazing. I never expected anything some…I'm not sure what to call it."

"This is my momma's secret garden. She worked on it for a long time. Rafe helped her some, because he's got a green thumb, just like her."

"You didn't help?" A mischievous smiled kicked up the corner of Maggie's lip with the question, her gray eyes twinkling in the glow of the fairy lights.

"I'm kind of forbidden to touch anything green. I'm good at a lot of things. Growing plants ain't one of them." He shrugged at the sound of her laughter. "I didn't inherit the gardening gene. My brother, Shiloh, didn't either. Dane tends more toward the vegetable garden than flowers, but he can make any vegetable grow. Nica's good with flowers. They seem to naturally bloom whenever she touches them."

"I've never been much for gardening either, to tell the truth. They're beautiful to look at, especially when they are planted and maintained by somebody who truly loves what they do. I much prefer the end result to all the hard work." Maggie spun in a circle slowly, her arms out from her sides. "Although if I had something like this, I might change my mind. It's peaceful."

"Yeah, it is. And, you should be honored. It's not everybody who gets invited to visit Momma's garden. It's a family thing, special, so most folks don't know about it."

Maggie's eyes widened at his words, before she crossed her arms over her chest, and drew in a deep breath. "I'll have to remember to thank your mother. This place, this moment out of time, is exactly what I needed today."

"You seemed to get along with Momma and the ladies. Heard you laughing quite a bit."

Maggie chuckled. "That's because I told them how we met."

"That you pulled a shotgun on me when I hadn't done anything to deserve it?"

"Yep. I think it was more the fact I surprised you than the gun itself. I take it you don't get caught unawares often?"

He hesitated for second. "I'm usually aware of who and what is going on around me. It's rare for somebody to get the drop on me. But you did, Miss Maggie. I never expected you."

That was the plain truth. He'd never expected to find somebody like Maggie, a woman who made him think about things he hadn't anticipated. Things like settling down in

RIDGE

one place, and not moving from job to job whenever he got the call. Leaving the DEA and focusing on building his security business. Building a relationship with one woman—her.

"It was pure luck. A few minutes and I'd have missed you, never would have known you'd been there." Color swept into her cheeks, and he couldn't help smiling at the flush of color. It made her eyes sparkle.

"I'd have been back. We were meant to meet, Miss Maggie. This way it was more…memorable."

Walking to the bench, he sat and patted the seat beside him. "Let's talk."

Her brow furrowed, giving her the cutest little lines above her nose, and he reached out and ran his fingertip lightly across them, feeling the softness of her skin.

"We are talking."

"You told me a lot about yourself this morning." When she closed her eyes drew in a deep breath, he quickly continued. "I think it's only fair I tell you my story. How I came to live with Douglas and Ms. Patti."

"You don't have to, Ridge."

Cupping her face between his hands, he smoothed his thumbs over her cheeks slowly, a gentle caress, and marveled at how silky soft her skin felt to his touch. "I know I don't have to. I want to. If you'd like to hear it."

At her nod, he reluctantly slid his hands away from her face, before he did something foolish. Like sliding his hands

129

into her hair, angling her face just right, and kissing her until she was breathless.

"Our mother was born and raised in Shiloh Springs. Went to school here, kindergarten all the way through high school. She was friends with Ms. Patti all through high school and after. Anyway, in her senior year, she met a guy. Fell in love. They dated all through her senior year, and they were going to get married after graduation. Apparently, they had it all planned out, at least that's what she told us when we were kids. Shiloh and I don't have a lot of those details, because we were young and she didn't like to talk about it much."

"It sounds like she was the typical teenage girl. We all tend to fall in love in high school. Most of the time it fades away into nothing, or there's major heartbreak that makes everything seem like the end of the world. It's almost a rite of passage, part of high school life." Maggie gave his hand a gentle squeeze to mitigate the harshness of her words.

"Well, her and our dad thought they had life all planned out. They'd get married. He would join the service, because that would provide a place for them. They'd be able to get by on his pay, and Mom would find a part-time job to do while he was working. The weeks before graduation were some of the happiest of her life. That's what she told us. Too bad life never goes the way you plan, right?"

Ridge wanted to spring to his feet and pace inside the gazebo, needing to move, do something, to crush down the well of emotions churning in his gut. He'd loved his biological mother so much, even now it was hard talking about her. Though years had passed, it was still hard remembering how she'd suffered through the pain, always with a smile on her face. It wasn't fair. She'd been good. Kind. Loving. Yet she'd been taken from him and Shiloh before they'd even had a chance to love her.

"Three weeks before graduation, Mom found out she was pregnant. It definitely wasn't planned, and threw a monkey wrench into their small wedding with their friends. Ms. Patti was going to be the maid of honor and my dad's best friend was going to be the best man. Instead, they decided to elope. The way Mom told it, they planned to drive to Louisiana and get married, spend the weekend in New Orleans for their honeymoon, and then be back at school on Monday."

"Something happened to change those plans?" Maggie's voice was soft, with an underlying sympathetic tone, as if she'd already guessed what he was about to say.

"Yeah, an idiot with a gun happened."

He heard her swiftly indrawn gasp at the ugly vehemence in his tone, and he scrubbed a hand over his face.

"Oh, Ridge—"

"No, I shouldn't have blurted it out like that. I still get angry, even though it was a long time ago." Staring over her shoulder and taking in the beauty surrounding him, he drew in a deep breath. "They drove to Houston, which took about three hours, and stopped at a drive-thru place to get something to eat, before finishing the drive to Louisiana. Decided to sit in their car and talk while they ate. If they'd only gone inside…"

"We'd always make different choices if we knew what the future held, Ridge. You don't know what might have happened if they'd gone inside. Things might have ended differently, or they might have been much worse." His lids lowered when he felt her hand cup his cheek, her touch like a panacea to his soul. It was the first time she'd reached out to him voluntarily, and he swallowed past the lump in his throat at how it made him feel. What it made him feel.

"You're right. I don't normally talk about this, except with Shiloh. And Ms. Patti, because—well, she's my momma."

"You're very lucky to have had two wonderful women to be your mothers. That is a gift."

"I know, and I thank God every day that Shiloh and I have Douglas and Ms. Patti. They stepped up without question, and took me and Shiloh into their home when Mom died." There, he'd said the words. He'd hinted around, avoiding saying the actual facts, though Maggie knew. He'd have to be blind not to have read the sympathy and understanding in her gaze. But he knew she understood, having lost her parents, too.

"A guy tapped on the car window, asking for money. Nobody's sure exactly what happened next, but there were shots, and one of the bullets struck my father in the neck. He died at the scene. Mom got hit in the shoulder, and they rushed her to the hospital. In all the confusion of paramedics and cops, she ended up being transported to the hospital without knowing what happened to my dad. They didn't tell her until the next morning he'd died. When they asked her about next of kin, that's when she found out. Quinn, that was my dad's name, lived with an elderly aunt because his folks ran off when he was a kid. When Mom called her parents to tell them what happened and ask for help, they refused."

"What? How could they?"

"Mom and her parents had a big blowup when she told them she was pregnant. They told her to get rid of the baby, or she'd have to leave. That's why they eloped, because Mom wasn't going to get rid of us, though she didn't know we were an us at the time—just a baby. Quinn already talked to a recruiter, and had everything lined up to enlist days after graduation. Their fantasy perfect life, was gone because some addict needed a fix."

Finally giving in to the impulse, he stood and walked over to lean against the gazebo's rail. His hands tightened around the top railing until his knuckles turned white. He started when he felt warm arms slide around his waist from behind him, wrapping him in a hug. A feeling of ease spread through him, diluting the anger and pain, and he breathed a sigh, wondering how such a simple touch could bring an aura of peace.

"I don't have the words to tell you how sorry I am, Ridge. It's awful to lose somebody you love, especially to violence. But I do know what it's like to feel the grief of mourning a lost parent."

"I know you do, Maggie. That's one of the reasons I wanted to tell you. Because I knew you'd understand. People sympathize when they hear about my situation, but you've lived through losing both your parents. It's always there. The grief fades with time, but you always remember how they touched your life. Wonder how different things might have turned out if they'd lived."

"I'm glad you still had your mom, at least for a while. Can I ask what happened to her?"

"When we were ten, Shiloh and I found out she had terminal cancer. Despite her family never making amends, Mom moved back to Shiloh Springs when we were eight. The people she cared about lived here and she wanted to come home. We'd been here for about six months when she started getting sick. Turned out she had stage IV pancreatic cancer, inoperable."

Maggie stayed silent, though he read the mixture of horror and sympathy that swept across her face before she could hide it. He wouldn't burden her with the ugly details of how much his mom had suffered, the weeks turning into months of endless tests, while the disease ravaged her body. His only happy memories revolved around the Boudreau ranch. It became his escape from reality. Douglas would take him riding on the weekends, and he'd race across the pasture, letting the wind blow away all the pain and anguish. He'd been a child having to deal with a reality no adolescent should ever endure. He and Shiloh had been lucky, because they'd had the Boudreaus, who'd rallied around and kept them protected from all the ugliness and made them feel wanted and loved.

"Our biological grandparents turned their back on her from the minute she'd run away with Quinn, and never relented in their harsh stance, even when we moved back. They wanted nothing to do with Mom or with us. Which was fine with me. I didn't need or want people like that in my life, though I wish they'd been there for Mom. As far as I'm concerned, they can rot. I don't acknowledge them when I pass 'em in the street. When they come to the Big House, which is rare unless it's a town function, Shiloh and I stay far away."

"They still live in Shiloh Springs?"

Ridge gave a strangled laugh. "Yeah. They consider themselves pillars of the community, though I doubt much of Shiloh Springs would agree. Always trying to one-up Douglas and Ms. Patti. It irks them that the town loves the Boudreaus and merely tolerates them."

"Who are they? Because I won't have dealings with people who treated their own daughter, or her children, in such a heinous fashion."

KATHY IVAN

"Calloway. Richard and Julie Calloway. Richard inherited money from his father. Man hasn't worked a day in his life, and he married Julie because she was the perfect trophy wife. Like I said, I want nothing to do with them."

"I don't blame you." Ridge smiled when he heard Maggie call his biological grandparents a string of names under her breath, a couple of them he'd never heard before, but from the way she said them, he'd bet she wasn't singing their praises.

"Before she died, Mom wanted to make sure we were taken care of. That we had a home with people who'd love us and take care of us. Momma—Ms. Patti—remained her best friend, always there for her, no questions asked. She and Daddy already had four foster sons living with them. Rafe, Antonio, Brody and Heath were already in the Big House, and they were a handful. But when Mom got sick, they didn't hesitate to step up and say we could live with them."

"I liked your parents when I met them, but now I think I love them. Not many people would open their hearts and their homes so easily."

Ridge smiled and pulled Maggie against his side, relaxing when she laid her head against his shoulder. "They are two of the most amazing people I've ever met. When there's a need, big or small, they're the first ones there to lend a hand, open doors, or pull out their wallets. I told you all of my brothers were foster kids, right?" He felt her nod against his shoulder. "Rafe was the first. Maybe he'll tell you his story someday.

We've all got stories to tell, most of them harsh and ugly, yet two honest-to-God miracle workers changed our lives by showing us what true love felt like."

He almost smiled again when he heard her sniffling against his shoulder. Telling her his story wasn't intended to make her cry, but at the same time, he knew he'd done the right thing in letting her in, revealing the events that made him the man he'd become from the frightened boy.

"You changed your name." Her words weren't a question, but a statement of fact.

"Shiloh and I both became Boudreaus when Douglas and Ms. Patti formally adopted us with our biological mother's blessing. Though it's a family tradition to change your name legally when you turn eighteen. You've probably noticed that all of my foster brothers are Boudreaus. Except Lucas. He kept his name, but that's a story for another day. Even if we hadn't had our name changed with the adoption, we'd have changed it as soon as we turned eighteen. For all intents and purposes, we are Boudreaus."

"That's astonishing and yet not surprising, after what you've told me about your parents. Somebody ought to write a book about them, to show the world there are still good people doing what's right."

Somehow, the more he got to know Maggie, the more she surprised him. She wasn't like most of the women he knew. The ones he dated and then walked away from, never investing his heart or his emotions. Superficial relationships with no feelings involved, the way he liked it. With Maggie, even though he'd only know her for such a short time, he knew it was different—because she was different. Unique and special in a way that slammed into him like a freight train at full speed, snatching his breath and left him reeling.

Was it possible that she was more than a job? A means to an end in solving a case? He couldn't allow himself to get involved with a mark. It could compromise not only finding the cartel's leaders, but it could cost him his job.

But standing here, with her so close, having bared his soul of one of the most painful times in his life, he felt closer to her than any other person in the world. This was dangerous, uncharted territory for him, but he knew it was already too late to change course.

He was in love with Mary Margaret White.

# CHAPTER FOURTEEN

Maggie walked out of her gym, sweat beading on her face, and headed to the kitchen. She'd worked out hard this morning, her mind spinning, thinking about Ridge. It had been two days since she'd opened herself to him, told him about Michael and how he'd died. She'd also thought long and hard about Ridge telling her about his life before going to live with the Boudreaus and becoming part of their family. Imagined how hard it had to have been as a small boy, losing his only parent to cancer, leaving Ridge and his twin all alone. Except they hadn't truly been alone, because they'd had Douglas and Ms. Patti.

But the thing that kept her mind racing, her feet pounding along on the treadmill, was what happened after she'd heard his story. Her impulsiveness. Or was it stupidity? Shaking her head, she reached into the fridge and pulled out a bottle of water, running it across her forehead. She needed to cool off in more ways than one, because every time she thought about Ridge, she relived that moment in the gazebo. The moment she kissed him.

The memory of her lips against his still sent her mind

reeling. His lips had been soft beneath hers, and she'd felt his jolt of surprise at her brazen act before he'd kissed her back. And what a kiss it was, heady and mind-blowing and intoxicating all rolled into one soul-numbing kiss. His mouth parted beneath hers and she'd swept her tongue along his bottom lip, feeling a tingle race down her spine, that tiny frisson of excitement coursing through her blood. She'd wanted to do this forever, from the moment she'd seen him standing with his hands outstretched beside her house.

She remembered his arms wrapping around her, his hand spreading through her hair, gently tugging at the strands as he positioned her to deepen the kiss, and she'd wound her arms around his neck, using Ridge as her anchor to the world, because she felt like she was floating, buoyed by the blissful sensation evoked by her mouth meeting his.

Their kiss was the most beautiful, perfect thing ever—and it had ruined everything.

Darn the man, he'd been avoiding her ever since *The Kiss*. A brief smile tugged at her lips as she realized she was referring to it in her mind with capital letters. Like it was something momentous. Probably because it was, at least to her. Guess it didn't mean anything to Ridge. So why couldn't she stop replaying it over and over again?

"Hey, Maggie, mind if I cut out an hour early?"

Felicia practically skipped into the kitchen and put the caddy of cleaning supplies under the kitchen sink. The happy smile lighting up her face made it clear she had better things to do than clean. Not that she blamed her. Earlier, Felicia told her about the new guy she'd been seeing. Turned out they'd been dating for about six weeks. Funny how she'd never mentioned him before. It wasn't like her friend to keep something like that a secret. It certainly wasn't her norm. Usually five minutes after Felicia met a guy, she'd be on the phone, telling Maggie every little detail. Maybe this guy was special, more serious than Felicia's usual hit-and-run relationships.

"No problem. Got a hot date?"

Felicia chuckled as she pulled off the smock she wore over her clothes when she was cleaning. Said she didn't like getting all dusty, and this way she didn't have to go home and change after she finished work.

"Yep. I'm telling you, Mags, this guy is different. He treats me like I'm special. Doesn't mind picking up the tab when we go out, never even asks me to go Dutch. How cool is that? And he doesn't take me to all the cheapo places like the losers I used to date. He treats me like a lady. I think he's the one, Mags, I really do.

Maggie couldn't help feeling happy for her friend. It was about time Felicia found somebody who treated her well. She'd been through a lot in her young life, and she worked hard to get ahead. It wouldn't be long before she graduated, and Maggie couldn't wait to see what life had in store for Felicia.

"Have a good time. I'm so happy you've found somebody special. You deserve it."

Felicia leaned against the counter, resting her chin on her hands, her blonde hair pulled up in a messy bun, and stared at Maggie. "You deserve to be happy too. How are things between you and Ridge? You doing the mattress mambo yet?" She waggled her brows to emphasize her quip.

Maggie rolled her eyes and made shooing motions toward her friend. "No. I don't know where you got the crazy impression that Ridge and I are anything but work colleagues."

"Maybe because of the way you look at him. Or the way he sneaks glances at you when he thinks nobody's watching. Honestly, could you be more blind? Tell me the truth—has he kissed you yet?"

Maggie felt heat wash into her cheeks, knew her blush gave her away when Felicia burst into laughter. "It's not funny. And to answer your question, I kissed him."

"No way! Seriously, you made the first move?" Felicia raced around the counter and hugged Maggie. "I am so proud of you. I never thought I'd see the day when you finally came back to life, girlfriend. Go for it! Ridge is a total hottie, and you'd be crazy not to see what could happen between you. I bet there'll be fireworks, because if the sparks between you are anything to go by, you're gonna set the house on fire!"

"Go, get out of here! Hugo's probably waiting for you, and I need a shower."

"See ya!" Felicia stopped long enough to grab her purse out of the closet before heading out the front door, leaving Maggie alone. Wondering if what Felicia implied was true. Did Ridge watch her when he thought nobody was looking?

Shaking her head, she gulped down the rest of her water and headed for her room. She definitely needed that shower, and she wanted to call Henry. He'd promised keep her updated on when he'd be returning, and so far, she hadn't heard a word from him, which worried her. It wasn't like him to disappear. Hopefully there wasn't anything wrong.

She stripped off her clothes and turned on the shower, adjusting the temperature to hot. After her workout, she needed to keep her muscles loose, and the hot water should help. Plunging beneath the deluge, she made quick work of cleaning up, because she wanted to make that call. Wrapping a towel around her, she walked into her bedroom, and grabbed her cell phone. Sitting on the edge of the bed, she pressed the speed dial for Henry and listened to it ring several times before switching over to voicemail. She left another message, telling him she was worried, and for him to contact her as soon as possible.

Ridge had headed into town earlier to handle something to do with an emergency with his company, which left Maggie free to deal with the cabins. She needed to do a final check and make sure they were ready to be occupied. There couldn't be any hiccups, not with something this important. In less than twenty-four hours, they'd be filled with people, and she refused to allow any screw-ups to derail something she'd worked so hard to accomplish. Nothing and nobody would keep her from fulfilling her word.

Not even Ridge Boudreau.

Ridge sat across the table from his brother at the coffee shop. Shiloh had sent him a message that he was in Santa Lucia, had driven in and wanted to see him. They'd always been close growing up, dealing with everything at a young age, until they'd gone their separate ways due to their jobs. Ridge had an apartment in Shiloh Springs, but more often than not he got called to work a job out of town, oftentimes across the country, as part of his DEA cover. Shiloh lived in San Antonio, working as a private investigator, and was rapidly climbing the ladder, earning a reputation for being one of the best in the state. He was proud of his baby brother, though he never let Shiloh forget Ridge was the oldest by a whole thirteen minutes.

"How long you gonna be around, bro?"

"Probably a couple of weeks depending on a case that's pending. In the meantime, I'm taking a break. This last case burned me out. It turned ugly fast." Shiloh took a long drink of his coffee, before adding, "I hate liars. Have I mentioned that?"

"All your life. Unfortunately, seems like that's all people

do nowadays."

"Tell me, dude, why'd you want to meet here? I figured I'd meet up with you, maybe crash at your place."

"You're welcome to it for as long as you'd like. You've got a key. I'm working a case, and I'd love to get your take on a couple of things."

"Ask away." Shiloh leaned back in his chair, studying Ridge's closed-off expression.

Ridge contemplated where to start. His brother was one of the few people who knew what he really did. He'd kept it on the down low, because if his cover got blown, he'd wind up unable to work undercover any more—or dead. He'd just as soon not have either scenario happen.

"We got a reliable tip a drug cartel is using a passage right here in our own backyard. I've been working with Daniel Kingston, trying to figure out exactly where the trucks are disappearing off our surveillance. They're funneling that crap onto the streets, raking in millions, and killing I can't even tell you how many people."

"That stinks. I can't fathom strangers' trucks loaded with contraband going through Shiloh Springs, much less the residents allowing it. But why are we *here*? Santa Lucia, Texas, doesn't strike me as the latest drug capital of the southwest."

"Our tipster implicated a local landowner, said she agreed to allow the trucks to cut through an unincorporated portion of her property in exchange for a share in the profits.

The land in question rides along both sides of the border, Burnet County and Shiloh Springs. Since I'm intimately familiar with the area, the DEA felt I would be an asset in uncovering the truth, and plugging the hole."

"She? You're telling me a woman is allowing millions of dollars' worth of illegal drugs to cross her land?" Shiloh shook his head. "Doesn't she sound like a peach?"

"Maggie's not like that. I knew from the moment I met her that she'd never allow anybody to run drugs on her property. It's not possible."

Ridge knew he'd given himself away when Shiloh leaned forward in his chair, a smirk on his lips. "Maggie? I take it you like this woman?"

"She's different than anybody I've ever met, bro. Feisty, intelligent, and doesn't take crap from anybody. First time I met her, she pointed a gun at my head."

Ridge knew he'd surprised his brother, who straightened in his chair, attention focused solely on him, where before he'd been distracted, only halfway paying attention. "Now I'd give anything to have seen that. My big brother stopped in his tracks by a pretty gal. I am assuming your Maggie's pretty?"

"She's beautiful. And before you think about it, she's not for you. Maggie isn't the one-night stand type of woman, and you're—well, you."

Shiloh scratched his fingers against the light scruff on his cheek, and Ridge wanted to squirm under his brother's scrutiny. Nobody knew him better than Shiloh. Maybe it was part of that whole twin telepathy thing, but his bro knew exactly what buttons to push to get Ridge riled up, and when to back off. Now was one of those back-off moments.

"I get that you like her. But what makes you think she isn't involved? People will do a lot of shady things for money, regardless of whether it straddles the lines of decency or not. Allowing safe passage for a drug cartel would net her a huge payday."

"That's the thing. Maggie's loaded; she doesn't need money. She inherited enough money, she couldn't spend it all in her lifetime. It doesn't fit."

"Okay."

When Shiloh didn't elaborate on his monosyllabic comment, Ridge countered, "Okay? What's that supposed to mean?"

"It means I believe you. Question is, how're you going to prove it before the next run goes through? Because I'm thinking if you're here, it has to be happening soon."

"That's the million-dollar question. I've been working on her security, going over the past logs with a fine-tooth comb, and I've found nothing. Zilch. Granted, a good chunk of the property isn't fenced or alarmed, so it's plausible that somebody is sneaking across her land without her knowing about it, but that's a stretch. Maggie hasn't done anything untoward, nothing to make me think she knows the trucks are going to roll any time now."

As soon as the words left his mouth, Ridge realized that actually wasn't true. The past two days Maggie had been acting antsy and distant, spending more time by herself, or disappearing for a couple hours without telling him. Not that she needed his permission; they weren't in any kind of relationship. Maybe it was part of her routine. Her comings and goings weren't any of his business—except they were, as part of the investigation. Like it or not, he was going to have to confront her and get some answers, before anybody ended up hurt.

"From the look on your face, you've thought of something, dude. Spill."

Ridge sighed deeply. "Maggie's been…different…the last couple of days. Disappearing for chunks of time, being more distant. I probably would have noticed sooner, but I've been a little preoccupied."

"Any reason, other than the obvious, why you've been off your game?"

Darn his brother, he'd always been so astute and tuned into Ridge's emotions. Couldn't hide a thing from his twin. "She kissed me. In the gazebo at the Big House."

Shiloh laughed, the sound ringing loud enough that other customers looked their way. Ridge sat stone-faced, waiting for his brother's hilarity to die. It wasn't funny, not in the least.

"Dude, you're a goner."

"It's not like that," Ridge protested.

"Sure, sure. It wasn't like that with Rafe. Or Antonio. Or Brody. They all kissed their gals in the gazebo, and look what happened." His brother's mood grew pensive, his lids half-lowered, obscuring his gaze, and Ridge found himself wanting…needing…to know what his brother thought.

"Do you love her?"

Ridge hesitated, wanting to deny the truth, but he couldn't. He wouldn't lie to his brother. "Yes. I don't know when it happened, but somewhere, somehow, I've fallen in love with Maggie."

Shiloh picked up his coffee and saluted Ridge. "We need to figure out how to clear Maggie's name then, so you can be with your woman."

"That's my plan. One way or another, I'm getting Maggie out of this mess. And I think I'm gonna need your help. You game?"

Shiloh gave him his patented *stop-acting-like-an-idiot look*, the one he'd perfected in his teens. "I can't believe you'd even ask such an asinine question. Anything you need, brother, I'm here for you."

"Good. Here's the plan."

Leaning closer, he told Shiloh exactly what he wanted him to do.

# CHAPTER FIFTEEN

Ridge decided it was high time he had a face-to-face with Daniel. His team scoured Maggie's property west of her house, which contained the majority of the unincorporated land, and they'd found nothing except for three tiny houses under a canopy of trees. He planned to ask her about them, because she'd never once mentioned having additional housing, and wondered why they were there. Did they need extra security, because they weren't included in her current alarm package? He knew, because he knew what she had and didn't have backwards, forwards, and sideways.

He wanted to be with her, but instead she'd taken off—again—right after her daily workout and breakfast. Didn't tell him where she was headed. Not that she had to, but the fact that she'd started disappearing each day without a word was grating on his nerves, and rousing suspicion. He'd convinced himself that she wasn't involved with the drug smuggling, and still didn't believe she'd do it. But doubt began creeping into his thoughts.

Knocking on the hotel room door, he waited, hands shoved into his jean pockets. Daniel swung the door inward, and Ridge strode through, taking in the almost pristine appearance. Bed was made, the curtains pulled open. A laptop sat on the table, with a stack of papers neatly piled beside it. Across the table, Roland gave Ridge a brief nod, before continuing to study whatever was on his own screen, frowning. Whatever the guy saw wasn't making him happy.

"Any news?"

Daniel simply stared at Ridge, as if implying his question was stupid. "I simply meant with Henry Duvall. He give up any more information?"

Daniel slowly shook his head. "Nope, he's been pretty close-mouthed since we picked him up. The most cooperation we've had outta the guy was when he made the phone call to Ms. White, giving you his blessing. But our team has searched Ms. White's property, and there is no sign anybody has or is planning to traverse a route there. Shoot, there's barely dirt paths wide enough for an ATV, much less anything the size of the pickup trucks and vans the cartel utilize to move their drugs. They found nothing except for the little houses I told you about. They're fully stocked and equipped with power lines, buried underground. Whole setup must've cost her a pretty penny, too. There's also camouflage netting strung between the trees. No clue why she'd do that, because it blocks the sunshine. Personally, I doubt they're set up for friends and family. Could be a stopgap spot for our bad guys though, to lose any surveillance if they suspect they're being followed."

"I think the netting might be to block the drones. Which make me wonder what she's doing with three tiny houses? She definitely doesn't need the extra space. Her house is huge, plenty big enough for guests. I plan to ask her about them today. I'm sure she's got a good explanation." At least, Ridge hoped she did, because he hadn't been able to come up with one.

"I checked the prices for those particular tiny houses, and those models didn't come cheap," Roland glanced at Ridge, making eye contact for mere seconds before going back to his computer. "From all accounts, each one runs between fifty and seventy-five grand. Add in the cost of running electricity underground, you're not talking chump change. Those houses are there for a reason. Whether nefarious or not remains to be seen."

*Nefarious? Dude, get a life.*

"Could the drivers be pulling onto Ms. White's land, hiding deep on the property, and staying a day or two, maybe more, until surveillance has lessened, and then continue on with the drugs? If she's got safeguards in place, like the netting, what's to say she isn't harboring these fugitives until it's safe for them to continue? It makes a weird kind of sense." Daniel resumed his seat in front of his laptop, and pulled up a topographical map. "Here's where we found the houses. They're small, but fully stocked with everything. Food, drinks, bedding. She's making things easy for these scumbags, and sleeping in one of those tiny things is probably a heck of a lot more comfortable than sleeping in their trucks or staying in a fleabag hotel." He shrugged at Ridge's glare. "I'm just saying."

Ridge studied the map, memorizing where Daniel had pointed. He'd driven that area on the ATV and hadn't spotted the tiny homes. Shaking his head, he gave himself a mental slap. He'd been too distracted, allowed his focus to drift, instead of doing the job.

Walking over to the window, he glanced down at the expanse of parking lot and shook his head. Even now he was distracted, itching to get back to Maggie, instead of keeping his mind on getting millions of dollars of junk off the streets. He started to turn away when he spotted a slender woman with long dark hair climb out of a van and head toward the bus discharging passengers. Was it—could it be Maggie?

Zeroing his focus on the woman, he sucked in a breath when he caught a look at her face. It *was* Maggie. Pulling aside the sheer white drapery, he leaned closer to the window, following Maggie's every move. He watched as she met with two women who'd disembarked from the bus with four kids. Maggie talked animatedly to the women, smiling and pointing toward the vehicle she'd climbed out of moments before. Within minutes, they'd loaded in, and Maggie drove away. He wondered where the van came from; he didn't recognize it from her garage. Questions were mounting, and he was determined it was time to get the answers straight from the source.

"Daniel, I think it's time I confront Maggie with what we've got. The runs taking place in the next twenty-four hours. We're out of time, and if she's part of this—which I still doubt—I'll bring her in myself. This ends now."

"Why the sudden change of heart, Boudreau?" Roland studied Ridge like he was some kind of bug under a microscope, with an air of fascination.

"Because I just saw her load a group of people in a van and drive away from your hotel. She's been acting secretive the last couple of days, and I aim to get to the bottom of this, once and for all."

Without another word, he headed for the door, but stopped with his hand on the knob. "When this case is over, I'm done."

"What? Wait a minute, Boudreau. You can't quit just like that," Daniel sputtered, jumping from his chair. "You're part of this team. You can't walk away."

With a smile, Ridge shot back. "Watch me."

Maggie's stomach clenched and rolled, and her palms sweated. Since Henry wasn't around, she'd have to do his job. He'd made a lot of the arrangements, dealing with their contacts, and making sure the finite details were covered. Or he did, until he'd gone out of town at the last minute, and hadn't made arrangements for pickup of the women and children. Without backup being arranged, she'd have to handle things herself.

She could do this. It had been her idea in the first place. When she'd first started contacting people, it had taken months of wading through organizations, dealing with social workers, finding people who pointed her in the right direction. What she was doing wasn't strictly legal—but it was necessary.

Now she sat outside the hotel, determined to see her plans through. Waiting. Hoping. Scared half out of her mind she was going to be caught and arrested. Up to this point, she hadn't done anything wrong, but once she met her contacts, everything would change. Maggie straightened in her seat in the van she'd bought a couple of days earlier. She'd forked over cash so it couldn't be traced back to her. She hadn't even applied for the title yet, because in two days, the van would disappear permanently.

Her eyes widened as she watched the bus pull alongside the hotel. It was one of those big luxury vans, with all the bells and whistles, the kind business commuters used when traveling from city to city within the state. It cost a lot more than a regular bus ticket, which made it ideal for her purposes. Going this route made it harder for the passengers to be tracked. They'd been booked under fake names, and paid for with a corporate credit card to a company buried beneath a multitude of dummy companies. Nobody looking for the women would think they'd pay extra to ride in style, which was exactly the point.

It didn't take long for her to spot her visitors. Two women stood, shoulders slumped forward, their posture defeated. One woman carried an infant who couldn't have been more than a few months old, and a little boy clutched her hand, his silky blond hair curly and mussed. A second woman held the hand of two young children who bore a striking resemblance to each other. Twins. She hadn't expected that, and her heart ached at the aura of sadness surrounding the small group of travelers.

Climbing from the driver's seat, Maggie walked toward the women. "Good afternoon. Are you Isabelle and Caroline?" She knew those weren't their real names, but simply part of an elaborate scheme to help these women and their families disappear with new identities. A port in the storm, she was a pit-stop on their journey of escape.

The darker-haired woman nodded, and glanced down at her baby. "Yes." Her words were barely above a whisper, but Maggie understood her hesitance, her reluctance to trust anyone.

"I'm Mary. Why don't we get your things, and I'll take you to the place where you'll be staying." She followed her words with a brilliant smile, hoping to convey that everything was alright, and they didn't have to worry about anything.

"Thank you."

"I'm glad to help."

It didn't take long to gather the few meager belongings they'd brought with them, and she winced at the threadbare duffle bags which contained all their worldly belongings. The kids piled into the van with little coaxing, almost as downtrodden as their parents. The van had been equipped with car seats for the kids and the baby, though the infant's mother seemed reluctant to part with the child even for a second.

She desperately wanted to stop and buy junk food and stuff them full, but she'd been warned to avoid doing anything other than picking them up and rushing them straight to the safe houses.

The ones on her property. The tiny houses she'd placed deep in the wooded area of her land, with every safety precaution she could put into place, including blocking access from anywhere, and keeping them camouflage from prying eyes. These families were on the run from untenable situations. They weren't criminals being hunted. They were abused and battered wives and children, trying to escape the unimaginable home lives they'd endured. Yet the very judicial system which should have protected them victimized them, granting sole parental guardianship and rights of these children to the ones who'd abused them.

"We'll have you settled in no time, I promise. I've got everything you'll need to last a few days. Plenty of food and drink. Clean bedding and a bathroom." Giving them an encouraging smile, she closed the van's side door and raced around to the driver's side. Time to get as far away from the bus as possible. In the improbable likelihood somebody spotted them, she'd lose them along the circuitous route she'd plotted.

Inside the van, it was unnaturally quiet, especially with four young children. Kids should be able to laugh and joke and play, not be silent and terrified, terrorized by their custodial parent. Shaking her head, she couldn't believe any court system could award custody to the abusive monsters that beat their wives and did even more unimaginable atrocities to their children. Kids were supposed to be protected and cherished, not used as punching bags—or worse.

The two women seated behind her were escaping their abusers, with literally the clothes on their backs and little else, except for the most precious things they possessed: their children.

Maggie remembered the first time she'd heard about the underground effort to relocate women who were victims of domestic violence and their need for waystations across the country. She knew they were all worse off than she'd ever been, but she connected with these women on a deeply personal level. Besides, she had the resources to help that so many didn't, and what good was the money if she didn't do something good with it?

The drive from town seemed like an eternity, because she had to circle around to the backside of her property, using the northern border to enter. She didn't dare use the front entrance. Somebody might see. Or their arrival would be recorded on the security footage, and she didn't want to explain to Ridge why six strangers had shown up on her property, only to disappear without a trace.

Meandering her way over the rough, rocky terrain made her go slower, but she finally pulled the van to a stop in front of the bungalows, as she liked to call them. Made them seem more like a vacation rental than a stop-gap. But no matter how much she prettied up the name, they basically were what they were: an interim port in the storm.

"Let's get you settled." Pulling the keys from her pocket, she unlocked two of the front doors, and let the women choose which one they wanted. Wrapping her arms around her stomach, Maggie watched as the woman with the baby, *was she Isabelle or Caroline, she wondered*, fingered the colorful drapes hanging over the kitchen sink. It almost broke her heart, and she couldn't help wondering what kind of hellacious life she'd endured that something as simple as curtains would be a big deal.

"Like I said, there's food in the fridge, along with snacks, sodas and juice. There's more in the pantry here," she opened the cabinet door, and watched the boy's eyes grow round at the site of the cookies and chips.

*Poor little munchkin.*

"Thank you. This is all…"

"You're welcome," Maggie squeezed the other woman's

shoulder. "I'll be back to check on you in a few hours. Let me know if you need anything." Opening a drawer under the sink, she pulled out a burner phone and handed it to the woman. "I programmed my number in there. Don't hesitate to call me, no matter what time, day or night, if there's anything you need or want. You are my honored guests, and I want you to feel comfortable." Glancing at the little boy, who'd plopped down on the sofa with some of the toys she'd purchased, she whispered, "You're safe here, I promise."

The woman's eyes filled with tears, and her mouth opened and closed a couple of times before she finally spoke. "Safe. I haven't felt safe in so long, I'm not sure I know what it feels like anymore."

"You will. Every day, it'll get stronger and stronger, until one day you won't remember the fear. You'll only know that you're never alone. There are a lot of us who've got your back."

The woman squeezed the burner phone in her hand, staring at it, and for a second Maggie wondered if she knew how to use it. Watched the woman run her thumb across the keypad, before she raised her head and smiled. "I know I've said it already, but thank you."

"You are welcome. Now, let me go and get your friend settled. You get something to eat. Give the kid a snack. And relax. Sleep. Do whatever you want; it's your life." Giving the woman a final smile, she climbed the steps and closed the door behind her, and headed for the next house.

Time to get the next family settled, and head back home.

And pray Ridge didn't find out what she was doing, because she didn't want to drag him into her web of lies. Hiding her activities from him had been almost impossible, and she knew it was only a matter of time before he figured it out and confronted her. She didn't want to lie, not to Ridge.

When all of this started, when the plans were made to provide shelter to these victims, Ridge hadn't been in the picture—she hadn't even imagined somebody like him existed. But he was quick, and he was smart. It wouldn't take him long to figure out her illegal activities, and when he did, she knew he'd walk away. He was too much of a straight shooter, a standup guy who'd never step across the line.

In her heart, she knew once he found out, any thoughts of building something with Ridge would blow up and she'd find herself standing in the ruins.

Alone.

# CHAPTER SIXTEEN

Huge black clouds hung low, threatening to burst any minute, and Ridge cursed as big fat droplets of rain splattered against his windshield. He'd raced to catch up with the van Maggie drove out of the hotel parking lot, but by the time he'd reached the front doors, she'd disappeared. Finding her now would be like searching for a needle in a haystack, so he did the next best thing. He called Shiloh.

"What's wrong?"

"You remember that plan we talked about? It starts now." Ridge swerved to avoid a bicycle rider who'd drifted into his lane, and he slowed down. Still in the middle of town, he couldn't hit the gas, no matter how much he wanted to speed through the streets to catch up with Maggie. Because he knew it was her he'd seen through the hotel room window. Nobody moved like she did, with a sensual grace that made his insides turn to mush. Nobody had the long chestnut hair pulled back into a sleek ponytail that bounced with each step. And nobody cried out to his soul the way she did, because his heart would recognize her anywhere.

"I'm on it. I'll head to her place. What moved up the

timetable?" Shiloh sounded almost breathless and Ridge knew his brother was running while they talked. He never did anything at half-speed; it was all full out or nothing with Shiloh. Ridge didn't like pulling him into this mess, but things were starting to spin out of control with the cartel and with Maggie. As much as he proclaimed Maggie's innocence, the odds were stacked against her, and he didn't trust anybody else to watch over her except his baby brother. He heard a car door slam and then the roar of an engine, and knew Shiloh was on his way.

"I had a meeting with Daniel Kingston and Roland Abernathy this morning at the hotel. While I was there, I saw Maggie. She was there picking up some people in a beat-up old van. I don't know why, but it's got my Spidey-senses tingling, so I need eyes on her while I'm not there. Looks like the cartel will be moving the shipment any minute, and I can't be in two places at once."

"Gotcha. How do you want to play this? Want me to stay outta sight, or pretend I'm there to see you and wait?"

"Bro, I don't care what you do. Use your best judgment. Just don't let her leave the house. Sit on her if you have to, tie her to a chair, but keep her there. She cannot meet the cartel today."

"I'm about ten, maybe fifteen minutes away her place. I'll guard her with my life, bro, I promise. Keep me posted."

"Will do."

He'd barely disconnected the call when his cell rang. Caller ID showed it was Kingston. Muttering under his breath and cursing fate, he knew what Daniel wanted even before he answered. The sky opened, and a deluge flowed from the sky. Thunder cracked, the loud booming sound shaking the car.

"Daniel, what's up?"

"The cartel's on the move. Like right now. The trucks are passing through San Antonio as we speak, so we've got about an hour, maybe an hour and a half before they're here. The team is scrambling, they'll be ready to head out in ten minutes."

"Son of a—I'm on my way." Ridge pressed harder on the accelerator, maneuvering through traffic, and wondering where in the heck all these people came from in the middle of the afternoon. Didn't anybody work?

The rain continued to pour as the skies opened and the daylight faded to darkness. His wiper blades barely kept up beneath the barrage, enough that he had minimal visibility. Thankfully, he knew the route by memory, having driven it so many times in the past few days.

"Ridge, you'll need to meet the team on site. We'll have people stationed on the road in front of Ms. White's property on the south side, and more on the north. Tracking them in this storm is going to be a pain in the butt, but we don't have any other option. If we don't stop 'em before they hit Burnet County, we'll have to start all over again, because we didn't find their hidey hole."

"You've got a tail on them, right?"

"Of course." Daniel sounded exasperated at his question, but Ridge didn't care. He wanted this case over and done. The flow of drugs through his home state, the freedom with which these mules seemed to run with impunity through the cities, made him sick to his stomach. He knew this one bust would barely make a dent, because every time they arrested the drivers, five more sprang up and took their places. It was like trying to kill a hydra: cut off one head and two more grew back. But this time, more than any other, it was personal—because of Maggie.

"How many?"

"Two trucks, pickups with customized camper shells. One dark blue and one black, very nondescript. We got three tails following them, standard formation, rotating out so they don't get spotted. But, get this," Daniel paused and Ridge wanted to scream at him to get on with it, "I just found out Diego Rivera is in one of the trucks."

"You're kidding! Has that been confirmed?"

"Oh, yeah. Got his pic captured on cell phone, sent by one of the tails. It's him alright."

Excitement surged through Ridge at Daniel's news. What were the odds of one of the top enforcers in the Escondido cartel riding into Texas with this latest shipment? It was like the gods were smiling down on their operation. If everything went right, this could be one of the biggest coups for the DEA in years, in addition to taking down one of the biggest connections to the Escondido cartel they'd ever managed.

"Boss, we've gotta make this work."

"I hate to ask, but what about Ms. White? Have you uncovered anything to confirm she's knowingly providing them safe passage?"

"Daniel—"

"Look, I know you like her. But, Ridge, you've got to do the right thing here. If she's innocent, it'll be proven today, and we'll offer her a most sincere apology when the smoke clears. However, if you haven't found anything concrete clearing her of wrongdoing, she's going to be hauled in with the rest of the Escondido crew."

"I'll do my job. I never let emotions cloud my judgment when it comes to taking down these scum. Not gonna start now." Ridge bit back the urge to tell Daniel exactly where he could shove the job right now. There'd never been a time in his life where he wanted to walk away more than right now—but he couldn't. Daniel would have no qualms about pulling Maggie in with the rest, exactly like he said.

Daniel sighed. "I know. This op ratcheted up into the stratosphere with Diego Rivera being on the truck, you know? He's slippery as an eel, and rarely crosses the border. I don't know what he's doing here, and I don't care. All I want is to throw him so deep in prison he never sees daylight again."

"Right there with you."

Rain pounded against the windshield, the sound reverberating inside the car, and a crack of lightning struck, close enough he could practically smell the ozone. Didn't it figure the one day they needed to catch a break, the heavens opened up and complicated things tenfold?

"You want to take the north side or the south?"

"I'll take the north. If by some fluke they make it all the way across the property, I want to be there." He didn't add *to stop them*, knew it was understood.

"This will work, buddy. See you on the other side." Daniel hung up, and Ridge prayed the man was right.

Maggie left the van parked about a quarter mile from her house, deep in the wooded area, and jogged back toward her house. She'd only made it about halfway before torrents of rain soaked her, and she shivered beneath its onslaught. Should she go back and make sure Isabelle and Caroline and the kids were okay? She'd just left them, but hadn't expected this downpour. Living in Texas, she was used to the skies opening suddenly with cloudbursts that lasted ten or fifteen minutes, but left enough rain to flood.

Picking up her pace, she clamored through the kitchen door, and began peeling off her shirt, squeezing the water from it. At the sound of a throat clearing, she spun around, finding Ridge standing in the middle of the living room.

Only something was off. Oh, he must have gotten a haircut while he was out. She wasn't sure if she liked it. Most of the time, Ridge wore his dark hair pulled back and tied with a piece of leather. In the evenings, when they'd sit out on the back patio, he'd take it down, and her fingers itched to caress it, feel the silken strands as she speared her fingers through it, pulling him in close for a kiss. Oops, that was her fantasy, they'd never done that—yet. She jerked the shirt against her chest, covering her bra, which was almost transparent from the rain.

"Sorry. I didn't see you there."

"No problem, sugar. I don't mind at all."

Eyes wide, she studied him, really studied him, because that didn't sound like the man she knew. The voice was the same, and other than the hair he looked exactly like Ridge. But he wasn't.

"You're Shiloh."

His lips parted in a blindingly white grin, and he shrugged. "Guilty. Though in my defense, I didn't expect anybody to walk in and start stripping."

"Where's Ridge? He didn't mention you were coming." She hadn't meant for the accusation to sound so harsh, but she was embarrassed. It wasn't like her to parade around half dressed, and it left her feeling at a disadvantage. Another feeling she didn't like.

"I'm not sure where big brother is. When I talked to him

earlier, he was supposed to meet me here. He even told me where the spare key was, in case nobody was home when I got here. I am sorry, I didn't mean to startle you. Can we start over? I'm Shiloh Boudreau, and I'm guessing you're Mary Margaret White?"

Maggie blew out a breath and swiped at the bangs plastered against her forehead. "Call me Maggie. Why don't you make yourself at home, while I go change?"

"Do you have to? I kinda like the drowned rat look. You pull it off beautifully."

She chuckled. "I doubt that, but thanks. I'll be right back."

"Sure. Want me to fix you something hot to drink?"

Maggie smiled over her shoulder as she walked away. "That would be awesome."

Jogging to her bedroom, she closed the door and headed for the master bath. Peeling off the wet clothes, she grabbed a towel and swiped it down her damp body, rubbing hard to get her circulation flowing. Yanking her hair out of the rubber band, she scrubbed the towel against her head, and then ran a comb through it and pulled it up into a messy bun.

Sitting down on the edge of the bed, she thought about the man standing in her kitchen, fixing her a drink. Shiloh looked exactly like Ridge, right down to the same crooked grin. Other than his hair being shorter, at first glance they were identical. Same eyes, same nose. Yet, Shiloh didn't make her feel inside the way she did with Ridge. When she was around Ridge, she felt excited, giddy like a schoolgirl, a teenager with her first crush. But more than that, she felt secure and safe from the world around her. He was a shelter, a refuge. He was home.

Eyes widening, her mouth dropped open in an "O" as the realization struck her—she loved him. She was in love with Ridge Boudreau. Accepting what she felt was real, she fell back against the mattress, laughter spilling from her. A kaleidoscope of emotions coursed through her, each racing through her body until she felt lightheaded, awestruck by the reality of acknowledging she loved him.

"Coffee's ready," Shiloh yelled down the hall, pulling her out of her revelry.

"Be right there."

She quickly finished dressing, and headed for the kitchen. Shiloh pushed a mug across the countertop, along with the carton of milk and the sugar bowl. Watching him, she couldn't help judging his movements against his brother's. Everything he did looked like an imitation of Ridge, right down to his hand movements. When she looked at his face, she noted his smirk.

"Sorry, it's just…you're so much like your brother. It's almost scary."

"Well, we are identical twins. Not surprising that we'd be alike. For the most part, though we are different in a lot of way."

"Really? How?"

"Well, for one thing, I'm better looking."

"Oh, please. Ridge is much more…" She caught herself before finishing the sentence, as warmth flooded her cheeks. "You are very sneaky, Shiloh."

"Guilty." He took a sip of his coffee, studying her closely over the rim. "You seem to know my brother pretty well. Should I be worried that you're going to break his heart?" All trace of joking disappeared from his tone.

"I would never hurt your brother. Ridge is the best thing that's happened to me in a long time. We've known each other such a short time, and yet there's definitely something there. At least for me. I don't know how he feels."

"Honestly? I think he's crazy about you. Which is why I have to make sure you're serious about what you feel for my brother. If you're not, end this now before it's too late. I don't know you, Maggie, but you don't seem like the type who'd toy with his emotions. Know this; if you deliberately lead him along and then break him, you'd better look over your shoulder, because I'll be there. That's a promise."

"Shiloh, I…" Before she could continue, her phone rang. The one she'd shoved in her pocket when she'd changed. The burner phone. "I have to take this."

Shiloh turned his back and crossed the kitchen, pouring himself another cup of coffee, while Maggie moved to the living room. "Hello. What's wrong?"

"Mary, I…I think the house is sinking. There's so much

water, it's flowing under the house. The kids are crying. Caroline is here with her children, we're all together, but I don't know what to do."

"I'm sure it's the rain. The ground can't soak it up as fast as it's coming down, so the mud might be messing up the ground a little bit. Don't worry, everything will be okay. It should stop raining soon, and everything will be great." *At least I hope so.*

"Okay…I'm sorry we panicked. When the house moved, the kids got scared, and I didn't know what—" Isabelle's words turned into a scream, and Maggie heard the shrill yells of the children in the background. Something was definitely wrong, and she needed to get there. *Now.*

"I'm on my way. I'm coming, do you understand?" When there was no response, she repeated her words, and finally heard a small hiccupping sound.

"I understand."

"Stay inside. Keep the children occupied. Maybe give them a snack or something. I'll be there as quickly as I can. I promise, it's going to be fine."

"I'm sorry to be so much trouble."

"You haven't caused any trouble. I'll be there soon."

Hanging up, Maggie spun around to tell Shiloh she had to leave, when she found him right on her heels. Dragging a deep breath into her lungs, she scolded, "Don't do that."

"Sounds like you've got a problem. Can I help?"

"Nope, it's something I need to take care of that can't

wait." Sprinting to the hall closet, she pulled out her rain slicker and shoved her arms into it. "Sorry to leave you alone, but I'm sure Ridge will be here shortly. I'll be back as soon as I can."

"Miss Maggie, I can't let you go out in this downpour. Whatever it is, it'll have to wait until this thunderstorm lets up."

Maggie stiffened at his use of her nickname. "Don't call me that."

Shiloh's brow furrowed. "Don't call you what?"

"Miss Maggie." She shrugged, trying to act nonchalant, while her instincts were screaming for her to move. "That's what Ridge calls me." She gave him a half-hearted smile to downplay the importance of the nickname. It might not mean anything to Ridge, but it was special to her.

Shiloh's expression lightened. "Ah, gotcha. Still not letting you leave the house though."

He folded his arms across his chest, and she took a single step back, her whole body going rigid at his words. Michael used to talk to her that way. Isolate her. Make it impossible to leave her home, kept her from having friends. Nope, she wasn't going to allow anybody to do that to her ever again.

"You can't stop me." Steely determination underlined her words.

"Whoa, sugar, hang on." Shiloh raised both hands to shoulder height, in a nonthreatening manner. "I didn't mean to ruffle your feathers, I simply figured whatever it is could wait until this storm passes, and the rain lets up a bit."

Closing her eyes, Maggie counted to five, and blew out a sighing breath. "Alright, I might have overreacted. But this can't wait. I'm not sure how long I'll—"

"I'm going with you."

"You can't! I mean, it's…you don't have to." Panic rose, her chest tightening. She couldn't let Shiloh come with her, because one, she didn't know him; two, he was Ridge's brother, and she doubted he'd keep anything secret from his family; and three, she couldn't expose him to what she was doing. It would make him complicit, and if they were caught, he might be arrested. It was too much to ask anybody.

"Maggie, calm down. Take a deep breath and relax. There's no way I'm letting you head out, not with this torrent of rain and the winds picking up. Not gonna happen. Either I come with you, or you're staying put. Your choice."

"Fine. I can't afford to wait. Understand this, you have to do what I tell you, no questions asked."

He looked her up and down, and gave a brief nod. "Let's go."

Maggie flung open the front door, and raced toward the garage, wishing not for the first time that she hadn't elected to have the garage as a separate building, instead of connecting it to the house. It was a mistake that she'd get corrected, because she was tired of ending up wet and dirty at the capriciousness of the Texas weather. Shiloh matched her step for step, and she punched in the code, opening the closest door.

Ducking inside, Shiloh let out a whistle when he spotted the cars and the Jeep parked side-by-side in the oversized building. Dang it, now she wished she hadn't left the van parked so far away. That thought quickly followed by the realization it probably wouldn't be the best vehicle to traverse the muddy terrain. Climbing behind the wheel of her Jeep, she opened the door to that bay while Shiloh jumped in the passenger side.

"Where are we headed, Maggie? I'm not prying, but I'd sure like to be prepared for whatever trouble we're headed into."

"I own a couple of small houses that I've got set up on the property. They're occupied at the present time, and there's apparently a problem. We're headed out there to see what's going on, and fix it."

"Small houses? Like bungalows or cabins?"

"Think more like tiny houses, similar to what you seen on television. The kind you can hook up to a truck and take with you. Small, compact, and easily transferrable from one space to another. The call I got said the house was, and I quote, 'sinking.'"

"It's on wheels?" At her nod, he continued. "Probably too heavy then. With all this rain, unless you've got a foundation or concrete slab underneath, the weight of the structure combined with the muddy conditions are probably causing it to shift."

"That makes sense. I never intended for them to be a permanent fixture." She slammed her hand against the steering wheel, before leaning forward trying to see through the windshield. The wiper blades weren't helping much, and the visibility sucked.

"Thinking about moving them to another location? Probably a good idea."

"Shiloh, I really wish you hadn't insisted on coming. Things might get a little…dicey, and I don't want to get you into something you aren't prepared for." Maggie stared straight ahead, partly because of the lousy visibility and partly because she didn't want Shiloh to read her guilty expression.

"Maggie, are you in some kind of trouble? Because if you are, I'll do whatever I can to help. Ridge trusts you, so I've got no problem trusting you, too. Tell me what's wrong, and let me help."

A loud boom of thunder rumbled, and it seemed to be right over top of them, quickly followed by a huge flash of lightning, illuminating the inky darkness. Maggie found herself praying that the storm would move through fast. Didn't it figure, the one time she did something outside the edges of the law, fate seemed determined to conspire against her, throwing roadblocks in her path.

"I'm doing something that needs to be done, trying to help some people get out of an untenable situation. But, and this is a really big but, it's technically a little bit…illegal."

She felt more than saw Shiloh's posture stiffen at her words, and she wished she could snatch them back, make them unsaid, but it was far too late.

"What part of what you're doing is illegal? Because I won't have anything to do with selling or distributing drugs. I'll tell you that up front; if you're involved in any way with putting that junk on the streets, I'll turn you in myself."

"No! What would make you think I'd be involved with drugs? I hate that stuff. I wish the government could get all of it off the streets. It's horrible."

He sat quietly, long enough she wondered what he was thinking. "Might be best if you tell me what I'm getting into. Just spit it out, kinda like ripping off a Band-Aid."

"About my tiny houses? Well, I set them up as a kind of waystation, a stop-gap for women and children escaping from horrific domestic violent situations. It's part of what you might call an underground railroad, because these women were married to men who had all the power and were able to obtain legal custody of the children. The same children they were abusing repeatedly while the supposed watchdogs turned a blind eye. Mothers who were downtrodden and beaten to within an inch of their lives, and nobody helped them."

"Okay." He drawled out the word, without any inflection, and she wondered again if she'd made a mistake bringing him along. If he decided to turn her in, she wouldn't be the only one going to jail. The women would be arrested, and the children returned to their abusers.

"I don't care whether it's legally right or wrong. I can't stand by and watch these women be beaten or raped, or kept virtual prisoners by the men who supposedly love them. It gives me nightmares when I think about what these kids have suffered. I don't think I have to paint you a picture of what they've endured in their short lives, do I?"

When Shiloh started laughing, Maggie's foot slammed on the brake. She whirled around in the driver's seat and shook her finger right under his nose. "Do you think this is funny?"

He leaned his head back against the headrest, and closed his eyes for a few seconds, before turning to meet her gaze. "No, there's nothing funny about their plight. I'm laughing because this is karma taking a big ole chunk out of my backside. I don't know what my brother's told you about what I do for a living. I'm a private investigator."

"He might have mentioned it. Why?"

"About six months ago, I was hired to work a case in San Antonio. Nice enough guy. A businessman, owns a couple of restaurants. Makes decent money, and he seemed like a straight shooter. He wanted me to find his estranged wife. Claimed she'd left him and took the kids. Not my normal kind of case, but he swore she was hurting the kids. Showed me the paperwork from the judge awarding him sole custody of his boys. I did my due diligence, checked for police records of domestic disturbances, looked into medical records. Two of the boys had been treated for broken bones, one a fractured arm and the other a broken ankle. Could have been the usual childhood accidents, but given the social worker reports, the legal custody awarded to the dad, I did my job and searched for his missing family."

Maggie turned in her seat until she stared out the window, watching the swishing motion of the windshield wipers at play across the glass, their rhythmic motion soothing, almost hypnotic. "You found them."

"Yeah. They'd made it all the way to Arizona before I caught up with them. Mom had a part-time gig working as a maid at a crappy motel for room and board, and enough to buy a few groceries. The manager said she was a good worker, reliable. He did remark the kids seemed like typical, happy boys, though they tended to stay indoors a lot."

"I'm seeing some eerie similarities here," she whispered.

"I called their father, let him know where they were. He had her arrested on federal kidnapping charges, and brought back to Texas. I swear, I have never seen anything like the faces of those kids when they saw him standing in the hallway of the courthouse. The hollowness, the utter defeat written on their expressions—it haunts me. I see them every single day. I knew I'd made one of the biggest mistakes of my life. This wasn't a loving reunion between a misunderstood father and the children he professed to love. No, they were his possessions."

"Exactly. I can't screw this up, Shiloh. These women, they're the first ones I've actually tried to help, and I can't even think about them getting caught and going back to the lives they've fled."

"I get it. I've been eaten up with guilt since that case. Funny, I've never told anybody about it, not even my brother. I guess maybe if I help you help them, I can atone for what I did."

Maggie reached over and squeezed his hand. "You didn't know. I've met your family, seen what a loving, giving home you came from. I had a good family too. But not everybody is as fortunate. Maybe if we help Isabelle and Caroline, we can make up for a tiny bit of the ugliness."

"Sounds like a plan." Shiloh nodded toward the rutted, muddy path. "Let's go make a difference."

# CHAPTER SEVENTEEN

A lthough it was late afternoon, all light was obliterated by the enormous black clouds rolling across the sky until it looked like midnight. Ridge had raced toward the meet-up on the north side of Maggie's property, intent on beating the trucks. He'd have to give them credit: moving their contraband during a Texas downpour made things tricky on their end, and gave the cartel the advantage of being able to move with less traffic out and about, with people taking shelter from the elements.

He bit back a curse as hail pinged against the hood of his truck. Great, like he needed another distraction on top of everything else. Hoping against hope Shiloh kept Maggie contained at the house, he searched the inky blackness for the other members of his DEA team. Some of them he'd worked with before, a few he'd never met, but they were all good men.

When his phone vibrated, he answered on the first ring, "Boudreau."

"We've got a problem." The strain in Daniel's voice more than the words told Ridge things were about to go sideways.

"What happened?"

"Our mark stopped outside of town. Diego Rivera got out and climbed into a sedan."

Ridge leaned forward, resting his forearms against the steering wheel, and staring out through the windshield. "Did you see who was driving the car?"

"Couldn't get a good look. All we know is it's a woman."

"Please tell me he's not stopping to get a little nookie in the middle of a shipment. That would be the icing on top of this whole lousy day." Ridge resisted the urge to bang his head on the steering wheel in frustration.

"They're parked on the side of the road, in front of an ice cream place. Can't tell what they're doing. The trucks have stopped too. We're playing wait-and-see. I want to get out of my car, go over and snatch his door open, yank him out and arrest him."

"Patience, grasshopper," Ridge joked. "He can't sit there forever. We're in the endgame here, and we're gonna take him down."

"I know. I'd simply like to go home to my wife and kid. It's been weeks since—" Daniel broke off, and Ridge straightened in his seat, anticipation zinging through his blood. "They're on the move, just pulled onto the street headed out of town."

"We're ready at this end."

"South team radioed in, they're all set," he heard Roland's voice respond. "Stay on the line, Ridge. I've got Rabbit and Maxwell posted on the south perimeter, half a mile past the entrance to Ms. White's land. Simmons and Baker about a mile past them, and Garner and Fitzgerald as backup." Funny how Roland sounded all businesslike and in control, nothing like the mousy accountant type he'd dealt with for the past few days. Ridge hadn't though the meek-mannered guy had it in him to take charge. Guess he'd read him all wrong.

Keeping the line live, he sat in silence except for the booms of thunder directly overhead and the pounding rain, splatting against his truck's windshield and hood. He'd shut off the wiper blades, cutting back on their distracting rhythm. He needed to stay sharp and focused. Right now, he knew where everybody on the north was positioned. He had double-checked their locations before parking his truck behind a large live oak, using its huge trunk and sprawling branches to obscure him from direct view.

Now it was a waiting game.

It seemed an eternity passed, though in reality it was probably only ten minutes, before Roland's voice came through on his phone. "The car and both trucks are approaching. Repeat, the suspect vehicles are approaching. They just drove past the entrance to Ms. White's property, headed west."

It made sense. Maggie's house faced directly south and the paved road ran east to west. Which meant they were headed in the right direction to access the undeveloped and heavily forested part of Maggie's property. Excitement coursed through him. This was it. Every instinct, every ounce of intuition, screamed today was the day. No more waiting and watching, trying to figure out where and how the drugs were crossing Shiloh Springs County and Burnet County.

It looked like the DEA had finally built a better mousetrap and the rats were headed directly for it.

"Keep your eyes peeled, Daniel. The motion sensors and the fencing stop about a mile and a half past the gate. Anything after that's fair game."

"Roger that. We gotta hope they—"

Ridge straightened up his seat, adjusting his seatbelt as the phone abruptly cut off. Tossing his phone onto the seat beside him, he clicked on his wipers, clearing the steady stream of rain off his windshield. Fortunately, it seemed to have lessened some, from a monsoon. Though still heavy, the torrents of rain were a heck of a lot easier to see through.

*Why wasn't Daniel calling back?*

The shrill ring of his phone nearly had him jumping out of his skin, and he grabbed it, hitting the speaker button. "What?"

"The car pulled over to the side of the road just past the turnoff, and the two trucks went around them and turned onto Ms. White's property. Simmons and Baker moved in behind them, running without lights. Stand by. I repeat, stand by, and keep your eyes open. Abernathy and I are hanging back, watching the car Rivera's in. Don't know if they spotted the tail on the trucks, but so far, they haven't made a move to follow or leave. They're sitting with the headlights off."

"We've got the north side covered," Ridge heard the first team he'd spotted when he'd pulled up.

"Roger that, boss man, we're here. They won't get by us." There was team two.

"I'm ready." Ridge answered, and took a deep breath. He was more than ready to end this case. Drive a nail into its coffin, and get on with his life. Even more important, though, was clearing Maggie's name, and proving she had nothing to do with running contraband across her land. He only prayed Shiloh managed to corral her and keep her at the house.

With the anticipation building, Ridge did the only thing he could.

He waited.

Maggie slid the Jeep to a stop in front of the tiny house. The electricity hadn't gone off, thank goodness, because the lights from inside shone through the curtains framing the window beside the front door. Shiloh was first out of the car, but he waited for her. She immediately gave him a tight smile, knowing the next few minutes might be more than a little tense. The women inside the cabin were skittish in the best of circumstances. Throw in being in a strange place with torrential rains battering the world outside their door, and add in a strange man? Yeah, she could see all the things that could possibly go wrong with that scenario.

She glanced toward the wheels and groaned. They'd definitely sunk a couple of inches deep in the mud, which probably explained Isabelle's thought that the house was sinking.

Change of plans. It was no longer safe for them to stay here. She'd have to load everybody up and take them back to her place. Not the ideal solution, but what else was she supposed to do, leave them here? Not happening.

Tugging her slicker closer around her, she pounded on the door, trying to be heard over the pouring rang and thunder. A pale-faced Isabelle answered the door, her son clinging to her leg.

"Everybody okay?" She was loath to step inside and track mud through the confined space, so she stuck her head inside the open doorway, and spotted Caroline and her kids sitting hunched around the minute table with its bench seating. It was obvious the children had been crying. Their eyes were red-rimmed, the half-eaten package of cookies in front of them sitting forlornly in the middle of the table.

"I'm sorry to be so much trouble. I…didn't know what else to do." Isabelle clutched the baby closer to her chest, never meeting Maggie's eyes. Her heart squeezed in her chest, knowing this woman had learned to expect the worst from life, and wasn't surprised when she didn't get her happy ending.

"You are no trouble, I swear. Nobody expected anything like this. The weatherman predicted some rain. I think he miscalculated how much," Maggie joked with a smile. "Here's what we're going to do. We are going to load everybody into my Jeep out there and I'm taking you to my house. There's plenty of room, hot showers, and food. It'll be a tight squeeze, but we'll make it work."

Maggie watched Isabelle start to nod, then she spotted Shiloh standing behind her. She took an involuntary step back, clutching the infant to her chest tight enough it let out an abrupt squeal.

"It's okay, he's here to help. This is Shiloh. He's a friend."

"Hello, ma'am." Shiloh was smart and didn't move any closer. Instead, he simply waved and nodded. Maggie knew if he was anything like his brother, he wanted to dive right in and take charge, but he stayed back, letting her run things her way. *Yep, he was a smart man.*

"Shiloh, why don't you go and open all the Jeep's doors, so everyone can stay as dry as they can?"

"I'm on it." He sprinted around the Jeep, and she watched the interior light come on. He even opened the hatch in the back. Good idea, the kids could scramble in there. It might be a tight fit, but they'd manage. He even managed to snag the old Army blanket she kept tucked in the back corner.

*Too bad I'm in love with his brother, because if I'd met him first…*

Whoa! Wait a minute. Did she really just think that? Her hand rose to cover her mouth, trying to hold back her laugh. Talk about bad timing. Here she was in the middle of a monsoon, with a sinking house full of women and children on the run from their abusers, and she couldn't stop thinking about being head-over-heels in love with Ridge.

"Maggie? Maggie?" Shiloh stood waving a hand in front of her face. "You ready to do this?"

"Yeah, let's go." Reaching up, she lightly took Isabelle's hand. "Let's get you out of here. Shiloh's going to hold the blanket over your head, so you and the baby stay dry. Go and climb in the back seat. We'll bring the kids out, let them crawl into the back. They'll be okay back there."

Without a word, Isabelle climbed down the steps and headed for the Jeep, while Shiloh walked beside her, holding the makeshift covering over her and the baby. After they'd settled, he came back, and did the same for Caroline. The three older kids didn't hesitate, racing through the rain and clamoring into the back of the Jeep. Shiloh pulled down the back opening, and Maggie sprinted toward the driver's side. Not that she made a lot of progress, because her feet sank inches deep in the mud with each slogging step. With a backward glance, she noted the tiny house had shifted further, the wheels buried at least two inches deeper in mud and muck.

Climbing behind the wheel, she headed back toward her house, driving slowly because she didn't want to bog down halfway back. She pulled onto the semicircular drive in front of her house and let everybody out, leaving the Jeep parked there. It wouldn't hurt anything to leave it out, and she'd move it in the morning. Right now, the priority was getting everybody warm, clean and dry.

Instinct took over and she directed everybody toward the extra bedrooms, assigning three of the spare rooms to the women and the kids. Taking a look at Shiloh, dripping all over her kitchen floor like a drowned rat, she put her hands on her hips and stared at him.

"Take the room down that hall," she pointed toward the hall past the living room. "Second door on the right. It's right next to Ridge's room. Grab a shower and get warm. He's probably got some spare clothes you can borrow."

"Think they'll be okay?" He jerked his head toward the upper floor.

"I think so. It's been a rather chaotic day. I definitely wasn't expecting Mother Nature to throw a monkey wrench into the works, but we'll manage. I'm going to make some sandwiches, maybe some chips, so they can eat. I'll fix you a couple, too."

Shiloh grinned. "The way to a man's heart, yada yada."

Maggie chuckled, and shooed him away. "Go get cleaned up. I'll grab a shower after you're finished."

"Maggie, you did great tonight. You kept your head, and because you did, it helped keep the women calm. What's gonna happen now?"

She shrugged, and wrapped her arms across her stomach. "I need to make some calls. I'd made plans for them to stay a day or two here, where they'd be safe, before moving on to the next place. On the other end, they've got new IDs, and people to help them get settled. It's all more than a little overwhelming."

"But you're making a difference. Once you've got this handled though, we need to talk. Because I can't let you do this again. Wait," he held his hand up when she started to protest. "You're doing a good thing, helping victims of abuse. I'm talking about the less-than-legal part of it. I get the feeling you care about my brother. I know he cares about you a lot. But having you on the wrong side of the law, even though your intent is honorable—it's not gonna work."

Maggie drew in a shuddering breath. "I know. I've been a total wreck this whole time. Worried about the women. Worried about the kids. Worried I wasn't doing enough. Worried that I'd get caught and ruin things for all the others working so hard to help. Every way I turned was a challenge and a nightmare rolled into one ball of nerves."

"I know some people who might be able to help. You and I, we're gonna talk. Once we get Isabelle and Caroline and the kids off on the next leg of their incredible journey, we'll figure out a way to legally and ethically help deserving women and men get the help they need. Agreed?"

Maggie felt her eyes fill with tears at Shiloh's unexpected offer of help. She'd never imagined in a million years that a stranger would step up. Though Shiloh didn't feel like a stranger. He was too much like his brother. The man who'd somehow, in such a short period of time, burrowed his way into her life and into her heart. She couldn't imagine her life without him.

"You okay?"

She gave Shiloh a quivering smile. "Yeah, I think I am. Go, get your shower and clean up. I'm going to fix some food for my guests."

Shiloh studied her, his stare intent. Finally, he gave a nod and walked away. Spinning on her heel, Maggie pulled open the refrigerator door, and started grabbing things to make sandwiches.

One crisis averted, but she had the feeling it was going to be a long night.

# CHAPTER EIGHTEEN

P atience was not his friend. Ridge drummed his fingertips against the edge of the steering wheel, and bit back the urge to scream. Yell at the top of his lungs, just to relieve the built up stress in the pit of his stomach. Felt like Mount Vesuvius about to erupt any second.

Somewhere deep in the woods, the two trucks wended their way from south to north, cutting across Maggie's land. Unless they stopped, unloaded their contraband and scattered it or tossed it away, the DEA had them. So, what was taking so bloody long?

Rolling down the window a small amount, he listened intently, hoping to hear the whine of a pickup engine. Something, anything. The phone remained eerily silent, except for the breathing of the two men on the other end, who hadn't remarked on anything for the last few interminable minutes.

"Rivera's car just turned into Ms. White's property, following the same path as the trucks." Abernathy's tone sounded almost gleeful. "We're going to take him down with the shipment, and cut off Escondido's right arm with

Rivera's arrest. Next best thing to catching Escondido himself red-handed."

Ridge studied the woods intently, as well as watching the roadway, glancing both left and right, in case the trucks came out further away from his stakeout position. He knew his other teammates watched various spots along the road too. They weren't getting away this time.

"It shouldn't be taking this long to drive across the woods. Something's wrong." The churning in his gut intensified, and he prayed he wouldn't end up with an ulcer before the takedown took place.

"Ridge, I'm sending the other two teams on the south side to meet up with you. Simmons is hanging back, but called in and reported they're almost to the end of Ms. White's property. You should spot them in the next couple of minutes. Roland and I are behind the sedan. Hopefully they're far enough behind Simmons they don't spot him or double back. I want Rivera caught."

"Team one, got it."

"Team two, we're ready."

"Team three, I'm in place," Ridge answered.

A tense minute pass, then another. Finally, Ridge spotted two lights about fifty feet away, moving closer. A spark of adrenaline raced through him, and he flexed his hands on the wheel. A dark-colored pickup pulled past the tree line and onto the roadway, heading east. Exactly as he'd anticipated, because east meant getting onto the interstate so the truck could head north. These little side trips through Shiloh Springs County and Burnet County had started when the Highway Patrol and local police had cracked down heavily on monitoring the interstate and I-45 through the Hill Country. Even though it was out of the way, and not a straight shot through the state, taking these circuitous backroads and small-town detours kept them off the official radar, literally and figuratively.

Ridge let the truck drive past, his intent focus on the second truck which was only a minute behind the first, headlights illuminating the night. About thirty seconds later, a car emerged from the darkness, and he spotted two men seated in the front.

"Daniel, you still have eyes on Rivera?"

"Affirmative. Tell me you've got the trucks." Excitement laced his boss's words, and Ridge grinned, feeling his own level of anticipation spiking upward.

"They just pulled onto the street, with Simmons right behind. If you've got Rivera's car, we're busting these jackasses."

"Go!"

Flicking on his headlights, Ridge watched the night sky light up with flashing lights as his team boxed in the pickups, with assistance from the south team, who'd shown up right in the nick of time. The drivers didn't even make a run for it, surrendering without even a whimper. Seeing the drivers in handcuffs, Ridge backed his truck across the spot where they'd emerged from Maggie's land, blocking the path.

In less than a minute, a car came barreling toward him at a high speed. Well, as high a speed as a muddy, rutted path allowed. The female driver slammed on her brakes, the car fishtailing and swerving before the front end slammed into a tree. Ridge spotted the talc rising inside as the airbags deployed, and flung his door open when he spotted the passenger door being flung wide, and Rivera struggling to get loose from his seatbelt.

"Oh no, you don't!" Ridge opened his door, jumped from the truck, racing across the dead branches and puddles of muddy water. He grabbed Rivera around the throat in a chokehold. He heard the muffled cries of the driver, so at least she was alive. He'd deal with her once he got Rivera secured.

Loosening his hold enough to allow the other man to breathe, he frogmarched Rivera over to his car and none too gently slammed him against the hood. Reaching on his belt, he grabbed his handcuffs and cuffed Rivera's hands behind his back. "Diego Rivera, you are under arrest."

Rivera spat a slew of curses, both English and Spanish, at Ridge, swearing vengeance once he was free. Right, like that was gonna happen.

Daniel's car pulled up behind the wrecked sedan, headlights bringing into focus the woman behind the wheel, and Ridge's jaw dropped. Because he recognized her. Aw, man, this was going to break Maggie's heart.

It was Felicia, Maggie's housekeeper, confidant, and best friend.

Roland wrenched open the driver's door, and pulled Felicia free from the wreckage, and she burst into tears. While Roland dealt with the sobbing woman, Daniel headed over to Ridge, who kept a hard grip around Diego Rivera's arm. No way was he letting him get away.

"You read him his rights?"

Ridge grinned and shook his head. "Nope. Thought I give you that privilege."

Daniel bared his teeth in a grin that reminded Ridge of a piranha, all sharp and pointy and dangerous. "Diego Rivera, you are under arrest. You have the right to remain silent."

Ridge half-listened as Rivera was read his rights, his mind still reeling over the fact Felicia was involved with Diego Rivera. It didn't fit with what little he knew about her, but then almost all of his information about the pretty blonde was secondhand that he'd learned from Maggie.

"Can you deal with him?" he asked Daniel, jerking his head toward Rivera. "I'd like a word with the woman who was with him."

"You know her?"

"Yeah. I've got a couple of questions, off the record."

Daniel sighed. "Like that, is it?"

"No. I barely know her. She's Maggie's friend."

"Oh. Oh! You're thinking she's the one who told Rivera's people about how to cross the property, gave them access. That tracks. Make sure you or Abernathy read her Miranda rights first though, even if you speak off the record. Gotta do this by the book. I don't want *anything* that might give this piece of garbage a loophole to slither through."

"I only want to ask her a couple of questions, boss."

"Go for it."

Ridge glanced left, watching as local law enforcement pulled up to the scene, having been called to assist. No jurisdictional toes needed to be stepped on here. He waved to his brother, Rafe, who was climbing out of his truck. Rafe would be full of questions, and he'd fill him in later, but right now he needed to talk to Felicia before they hauled her away.

"Abernathy."

"Boudreau. Good job back there."

"Thanks. Have you read the young lady her rights?" He nodded toward Felicia, who sat swiveled around in the driver's seat softly crying, cradling her left arm against her chest, her right wrist handcuffed to the steering wheel. Her long blonde hair was plastered against her head, the track of tears streaked down her powder-encrusted face. Maggie would have had a heart attack if she could see her friend looking like this, terrified and defeated. Rafe, on the other hand, couldn't afford to be sympathetic or lenient.

"She's been mirandized, and I've made her as comfortable as I can. EMTs are on the way. How's Rivera, he hurt?"

"Doesn't seem to be. Daniel read him his rights, but I

doubt he's gonna spill his guts. Bet he lawyers up the second he hits the station."

Ridge glanced at Felicia again, looking so forlorn, her shoulders hunched and curled inward. Taking a couple of steps forward, he knelt in front of her.

"Felicia?"

Her gaze rose slowly and met his. Recognition sparked in her eyes. Opening and closing her mouth a couple of times, she gave a mocking laugh. "Guess I really screwed up."

"Guess you did. Roland tells me he read you your rights. Do you understand them? I'd like to ask you a question. Off the record," he added, because what he wanted to know didn't really affect the case; they'd got her dead to rights.

Felicia studied him intently, her eyes blinking slowly, before she finally nodded. "Go ahead, ask away."

"Why would you do this to Maggie? You're her friend. She trusted you."

"Because I'm a fool. I let myself be swept away with Diego's charm. He treated me like a princess. Honestly, I didn't have a clue who he was, not at first. When I figured it out, it was too late, I was in love with him. Deeply, madly, over-the-moon in love."

"Were you the one who showed him how to cross through Maggie's land? How to avoid the security system?"

Felicia nodded and choked back a sob. "I know you won't understand. When he first asked, I said no. I didn't want to hurt Maggie. She's my best friend. But he kept asking, kept pushing. He even tried seducing me into doing it. Finally, he offered me money. A lot of money. Enough for me to pay for my classes at the college and quit working one of the part-time jobs I needed just to keep a roof over my head. You're a Boudreau, you don't know what it's like to have nothing, to have to scrape and plead for every scrap."

Ridge didn't even attempt to argue the point. It sounded like she was trying to justify her actions, explain away why she'd betrayed years of friendship from a woman who'd have given Felicia anything she wanted if she'd known. Instead, she'd betrayed her in a heinous way, one sure to make Maggie feel as if the relationship she'd built with the other woman meant less than the dirt she ground beneath her heel. Being poor didn't excuse what Felicia had done, probably why she was trying to justify her actions, because the guilt rode her hard.

"I never wanted to stay in this town, but I was stuck. Don't you see—until Diego promised me enough money, I'd never have to scoop another ice cream cone or clean somebody else's house again. All I had to do was turn off the security system for a small portion of Maggie's land." She gave a defiant shrug, though she stared past his shoulder, refusing to meet his eyes. "I wasn't hurting anybody. All they did was drive through a shortcut. There's nothing illegal about that." The heated glare she shot him didn't mitigate the guilt he read in her expression. Not one little bit.

"Actually, it was illegal. It's called trespassing. What

about Maggie? Did she know about your deal with Diego?"

"Ha! That's rich! Maggie's so clean, she squeaks. She'd never look the other way. I swear, she doesn't know anything about what I did. Leave her out of this. Throw the book at me, I don't care anymore, but Maggie didn't know anything."

"Thank you, Felicia. The EMTs are here. They'll take a look at your arm and get you fixed up." He turned and started to walk away, when she called out to him.

"Ridge? Tell her…tell Maggie I'm sorry. I didn't want to hurt her."

Without another word, he maneuvered his way past the approaching paramedics, and walked over to Rafe, who stood talking with Daniel while a belligerent Diego Rivera cursed a blue streak and demanded his lawyer. He chuckled softly when Rafe told Rivera to shut up, he could talk to his lawyer when they got to the sheriff's station.

"Hey, bro. Looks like you missed all the excitement."

Rafe gave him an assessing look. "You got to have all the fun."

"That's because I did all the heavy lifting. You're welcome to the cleanup detail."

"Tessa's not gonna be happy. We had a date tonight."

Ridge chuckled. "In this storm? Momma wouldn't have let either of you leave the house. You'd have been stuck at the Big House watching movies or something with the rest of the family."

"That was the plan anyway, bro. Didn't you get the invite?"

"I've been kind of busy, tracking drug shipments and bringing down Mexican cartels. I'm sure Momma and Dad will understand."

Rafe slapped him on the back, hard enough Ridge stumbled a step. "Lucky me. Since you technically made the bust in my county, I get to deal with all the paperwork. Not to mention the moaning and complaining from this dude. Couldn't you have managed to bust these jerks in Burnet?"

"It is what it is, bro. I'll meet you at your office. I need to make a couple of calls first."

"Don't take too long. Your boss seems anxious to wrap things up." Rafe looked his brother up and down, his eyes glinting in the flashing strobe lights from the police cars, and Ridge knew his big brother wasn't thrilled he'd kept things from him. "I think you and I have some talking to do, mostly about why you didn't tell me about your side job. The one with the DEA. Might've been nice to have a head's up that my brother was working with the government, instead of finding out about it like this."

Ridge shrugged and gave him a sheepish grin. "What can I say, bro? I was undercover, my identity a secret. Do you know how hard it was, working a case in my own backyard, and not being able to tell anybody? Well, except Shiloh, because I can't hide anything from my twin. Dude's like a human lie detector; he had the truth out of me in under five minutes. I swore him to secrecy, which wasn't easy, because he doesn't like to keep anything from Momma. Oh, yeah, Antonio knows because we had a case that overlapped. Otherwise, he'd still be in the dark too."

"Go make your calls. I'll see you at the station."

Ridge watched as the paramedics led Felicia out of the woods, Roland sticking to her side like glue. It was funny how the meek pencil pusher came alive under the pressure of the takedown. He'd been all business, dealing with the aftermath, and with Felicia and her injury. Guess there was more to the guy than Ridge first thought.

As the paramedics loaded Felicia in the back of their unit, Roland motioned to Ridge, who jogged over. "I'm going to the hospital with her. They want to check for other injuries, but they're pretty sure her wrist is shattered. I suspect Daniel will have Diego Rivera checked out, since he was involved in the accident too."

"Probably. Good job, Abernathy...Roland."

"Thanks. It was more intense than I anticipated, being out in the field."

"It has its moments. Gotta go. I'll meet you at the Shiloh County Sheriff's Office later."

"Meet you there." He turned to go and Ridge remembered something he needed to tell him.

"Hey, could you give Daniel a message? Tell him I heard back from Gizmo about the drone we sent him. Turns out it had nothing to do with our case. The owner of the property on the other side of Maggie got it from a friend, who's working a project with drone technology. Apparently, the neighbor is friends with the developer, who gave him a working prototype of his design. The neighbor's kid was fooling around with it, and flew it over Maggie's land."

"Huh. All that worry was over a toy?"

Ridge grinned at Abernathy's disgruntled expression. "It's a little more complex than a toy, but, yeah, turns out it was a dead end. Gizmo thinks the developer is on to something, has some cool technology he's incorporated, but overall, it has nothing to do with the DEA's case."

"I'll let him know."

"Thanks."

Roland nodded and climbed into the back of the ambulance, which sped away, lights flashing and sirens blaring. Ridge drew in a deep breath and lifted his face to the sky. The rain had devolved to a soft sprinkle, the torrential downpour dissipating and he saw the moon peeking out from behind a cloud.

Climbing into the cab of his pickup, Ridge dialed Shiloh's number. He answered after the second ring, sounding breathless.

"Hey, man, how'd it go?'

"First, how's Maggie? Everything okay there? Did she give you any trouble?" Ridge spat out the questions in rapid-fire succession, barely pausing for breath.

"She's fine. We had a bit of excitement earlier, but I'll let her tell you about it. Did you get the bad guys?"

"That and more. It's been one heck of a night, and it's not over yet. I'm going to have to head to the sheriff's department, and get everybody booked and all the paper-work done. But at least we've got proof that Maggie wasn't involved."

Ridge heard his brother mutter something under his breath. "What was that?"

"Nothing," Shiloh answered. "Maggie gave me a room for the night, so I'll keep an eye on things, so don't worry."

"Good. We should have everything wrapped up by morning. I do have to talk with her about something we found out, but it can wait until I get home."

*Home? How'd I let that slip out? And when did I start thinking about Maggie's house as home?*

"No worries. I've got it covered. Bro, I've gotta say, I really like your Maggie. She is one special lady."

Ridge felt a gentle squeeze in his chest. His brother's opinion meant everything. Knowing Shiloh liked Maggie filled a void inside he hadn't even known was there. His fervent wish was Maggie felt the same way he did, because he loved her with everything in him.

"She's one of a kind." Even as he spoke, he noticed Daniel handing Diego Rivera off to Dusty, who assisted him into the back of his squad car. Time to get his head back into the job. The faster they got things wrapped up, the faster he could get back to Maggie.

"Gotta go. Tell Maggie I'll see her in the morning."

"You've got it. I'll see you in the a.m., dude."

Ridge hung up, and started the car. A thrill of accomplishment swept through him, knowing they'd put a big dent in the Escondido cartel. It wasn't the end, not by a long shot. But at least for now, one of the big dogs had been taken down, and they'd taken a couple of truckloads of illegals off the streets.

It was over.

# CHAPTER NINETEEN

M aggie watched as the two SUVs pulled out of her drive, the kids waving at her from the windows. She'd been on the phone before sunrise, contacting the helpers on her list, the people who'd step up in case of emergency—and if last night's fiasco didn't qualify, she didn't know what did—and made arrangements to get Isabelle and Caroline and the children safely on their way to the next safe house.

She swallowed past the lump in her throat, at their little faces pressed against the glass, even though it was only for a second. All her planning, taking every precaution she could think of, she'd still screwed up. The only bright side—knowing both families moved on with precautions and safeguards in place to get them to their next destination unscathed.

Turning, she started back into the house, but heard the sound of a vehicle coming up the drive, and saw Ridge behind the wheel. She couldn't help noting that he looked tired. With everything happening last night, she'd barely had time to notice he hadn't come home.

*Home. Somehow it feels right to think about Ridge belong-*

*ing here. With me. If only I knew he felt the same about me—*
*about us. I love him so much.*

He stepped from the car and climbed the steps. Without thinking, she opened her arms, and he stepped forward, allowing her arms to wrap around him. Putting her head against his shoulder, she let out a sigh, relaxing, feeling as though her world had righted itself on its axis.

After several moments of silence, Ridge stepped back, and smiled down at her. "Thank you, sweetheart. You've got no idea how much I needed that."

"Rough night?"

Looping his arm around her shoulders, he led her into the house. Maggie had to admit, she loved the feel of his arm around her. There was an intimacy in his touch that made her feel wanted. Even without a word spoken, she felt a depth of emotion from the simple show of affection. She wasn't sure he even realized he was touching her, yet whether it was intentional or not, it gave her a feeling of implied trust and caring.

They walked to the kitchen, and she patted one of the stools. He wearily sank onto it, while she walked around the counter and headed for the coffee maker. Popping in a pod, she chose one of the darker roasts. Ridge looked like he needed the extra boost of caffeine this morning. She didn't want to pry, but she couldn't help wondering where he'd been all night, and why he'd come home looking like he'd been run over by an eighteen-wheeler.

"Here," she said, pushing the mug toward him. "You look like you need this."

"Thanks." He took a sip and she watched a little smile curl up his lip, before his gaze met hers. "Miss Maggie, we need to talk."

*Uh-oh. Does he know what I did? How did he find out?*

"Yes, we do. I know I should have told you, but—"

"Shh. Let me go first."

"But I want to tell you about…"

"Maggie, I work for the DEA."

He watched her closely, studying her face like he was waiting for something, though she wasn't sure precisely what. "Um, okay?"

"Just okay? Aren't you wondering what a DEA agent is doing in your house?"

"I thought you installed security systems."

Ridge smiled, his eyes twinkling in the sunlight streaming from the kitchen window, before his expression turned serious. "I do. But that's not why I've been in your home. Maggie, sweetheart, you've been under investigation by the DEA."

"I—I don't understand. I have never had anything to do with illegal drugs. Heck, I don't even like to take aspirin. Why in the world would the DEA be investigating me?"

Ridge cradled the mug between his hands, and for a second, he looked so lost Maggie wanted to hug him again. Sometimes, at the strangest moments, he'd have these moments where he looked vulnerable and insecure, and she felt the urge to wrap him within a blanket of her love and let him know everything would be alright. Instead, she crossed her arms around her middle, waiting for his answer, because none of this made sense. The DEA investigating her? Never in a million years had she expected that response.

"We've been monitoring drug shipments from Mexico through this area for the past six months or so. The Escondido cartel runs illegal drugs through South and Central Texas. Some of the worst stuff you can imagine. Cocaine, heroin, you name it, they've smuggled it into the country. We got a tip from a reliable source that the cartel was using your property."

"No. Absolutely not. How could you even think that I'd allow something like that to happen here?"

"I didn't believe it, Maggie. Not from the moment I met you, with your shotgun pointed at my head. Even then, I knew you'd never allow it. Unfortunately, the DEA doesn't go by gut instinct. They needed solid proof. This is where I need to make a confession. I don't know Henry Duvall. The DEA picked him up and asked for his cooperation. He was reluctant at first, but they were able to convince him to help. Having Henry call you, and recommend me and my services was the perfect excuse for me to be in your home."

"Henry? Is he okay?"

"He's fine. Right now, he's in Maui enjoying the sunshine and piña coladas on the beach on the department's dime."

"I guess that explains why he hasn't answered any of my calls."

Maggie took a couple of steps forward, and leaned her hip against the counter, shaking her head at her naïveté. She'd bought Ridge's act hook, line, and sinker from the first day, barely questioning his sudden appearance in her life. "So, all of this was a sham, a way to determine if I was running drugs?"

"Yes…no…I never thought you personally were involved with the drugs. We were told there was a place on your land where the vehicles transporting the illegal merchandise would detour from the interstate. That's what I've been doing late at night and early in the mornings. Trying to find the passthrough the drivers took."

"Did you find it?" Maggie couldn't keep the bitterness out of her voice. Her heart was slowly breaking with each word out of Ridge's mouth. It had all been an act. A way to ingratiate himself into her world. Into her life. Had he ever cared for her at all, or was that all part of his undercover sting?

"Last night. We had surveillance on the north and south sides of your property, and caught the drivers and the trucks. Close to two point five million dollars' worth of illegal drugs. We also captured one of the head men in the Escondido cartel, Diego Rivera. That was an unexpected bonus."

She drew in a deep breath and started to turn away,

barely holding onto her last shred of self-respect. How much more could she take? Each word stabbed like a knife to her heart, and she wanted to crawl into a dark corner and hide away until all the pain was gone. Until Ridge left, because seeing him, knowing he'd never cared about her, that she'd simply been a means to an end, felt like a death blow to her very soul. She'd given him everything, told him about her deepest, darkest moments, and now regret and shame filled her. Once she had time to think, she knew the regret would turn to anger, but she wasn't there yet. Right now, all she felt was—hurt.

"Now you know I had nothing to do with drugs or the cartel or anything to do with your bust. Guess you'll be leaving. Or am I still under suspicion?"

"Maggie, we know you weren't involved. But somebody you know was; they provided the information about your land to Rivera. They turned off the security system while the trucks rolled through, restarted them when they left. I'm so sorry."

"Who?" Her voice broke on the single word.

"It was Felicia."

"What? No! She wouldn't! Ridge, she's my best friend."

Ridge's arms wrapped around her, even as Maggie struggled, striking at him over and over. A million questions spiraled through her mind, racing with blinding speed, tumbling in a chaotic swirl. She heard sobbing and realized it came from her.

Ridge slid to the floor, cradling her in his lap, and she wept at the betrayal of her trust and her friendship. She'd lost everything in one fell swoop—her best friend, her faith in others, and the man she loved. Could it get any worse?

"My Maggie, I'm so sorry. I'd give anything for you not to hurt so much. Sweetheart, please don't cry. You're breaking my heart."

"I'm not. I was just a job to you. A means to an end."

"No, Maggie. It stopped being a job the minute I met you. I knew in my heart you were innocent. You're a lot of things, Maggie. Intelligent, opinionated, feisty, and sarcastic."

She sniffed at his characterization. "Gee, thanks, I sound like a real pearl."

"Shh, I'm not finished. You're also caring, loving, giving. Everything you do, you do with your whole heart. There is no way you'd be involved with anything that would hurt others. But, sweetheart, my knowing it and being able to prove it were two entirely different things."

She struggled to sit upright. "You could have simply asked me."

Ridge shook his head, and cupped the back of hers, resting his forehead against hers. "That's not the way it works. My objections were overridden, and I knew the only way to make this all go away was to prove your innocence. Which meant I had to figure out who was guilty, because the one thing I did know was somebody gave the Escondido cartel specific instructions on when and how to cross your land. But never, for one second, did I think you did it. Not after meeting you. Getting to know you." He pulled back and stared into her eyes, and she nearly gasped at what she saw in his gaze. "Falling in love with you."

"You…you love me?"

The corners of his lips quirked upward, and he gently brushed the hair off her cheek. "How could I not fall in love with you, Maggie Mine? You're perfect—"

"I'm not!"

"You're perfect for me. I never thought I'd find anybody who fits me so completely. I never wanted a doormat or a fragile flower. Can't stand the Barbie-doll type. While everybody else might be looking for a quick one-night stand, that isn't me. I want somebody strong. Independent. Thinks for herself. Beautiful. Isn't afraid to speak her mind, even when it's something I don't want to hear. Compassionate. A fighter. In other words, I was looking for you. I love you, Mary Margaret White."

Tears filled her eyes, threatening to overflow, as she studied his face, reading the truth in his words. "I love you too, Ridge Boudreau. This is crazy. We're crazy. We barely know each other."

"Not true. We may have only known each other a short time, sweetheart, but we know each other intimately, in ways nobody else does. You know my secrets. I know yours. In spite of, or maybe because of that, we've found a love that's truer, deeper, and I believe it's going to last."

She gave him a trembling smile. "I do love you, Ridge. I honestly love you. My heart was breaking, thinking about you finishing your case, your job, whatever you want to call it, and moving on to your next assignment."

Ridge shifted until his back was against the counter, and she laid her head against his shoulder, her hand rubbing soft circles on his chest. How had their dynamic shifted on its axis in a matter of seconds? She'd gone from excruciating loss, her heart breaking, until now she felt as light as air, filled with a happiness she hadn't felt in—forever.

"I told my boss this was my last assignment. I'm leaving the DEA, and I'm going to focus my attention on my security work." He smiled at her, and she wanted to melt into a puddle. "I really am good at it. My company is the real deal, not a fabricated cover, in case you're wondering."

"So, you'll be sticking around?"

He leaned over and brushed a soft kiss against her lips. "I'm not going anywhere, unless you're going with me. I have an apartment in Shiloh Springs. It's sat empty a lot, but…"

"Stay here with me." The words rushed out of her mouth before she could stop them. "I mean, if you're serious about leaving the DEA, about living in Shiloh Springs. You said you love me, so…"

She stopped talking and felt a wash of heat in her cheeks. What was wrong with her? She'd never been this forward in her life, had never even slept with anybody except her deceased husband, yet here she was, asking Ridge to move in with her."

Ridge's slow wolfish grin had her squirming, but he kept his arm secured firmly around her shoulders, his eyes twinkling in the sunlight spilling through the kitchen windows. "Miss Maggie, are you asking me to live with you?"

Mutely, she nodded. He slid a fingertip beneath her chin, tilting her head up until she met his gaze. "Darlin', I'm not going to live with you."

She drew in a sharp breath, and opened her mouth to speak, but he placed a gentle finger against her lips. "I'm not going to live with you—I'm going to woo you. I'm going to make you see yourself exactly how I see you, as a precious gift that I'll never be worthy of receiving. Then, when I've convinced you I can't live without you, I'm going to marry you."

*Marry me? He wants to marry me?*

"Yes, love, I want to marry you."

Realizing she'd said the words out loud, she ducked her head again, and felt a stir of hope deep inside. Her every wish, every desire, every longing rolled into one, personified in Ridge Boudreau. How had she gotten so lucky?

"You don't have to convince me, cowboy. I am so head over heels in love with you I'd marry you tomorrow if you asked me. Shoot, I'd marry you today if we could get a license."

"I'd take her up on it before she changes her mind, bro."

Maggie jumped at the sound of Shiloh's voice, and peered upward to see Ridge's twin standing on the other side of the counter. She'd all but forgotten he'd spent the rest of the night, after helping her get the women sorted out and on their way. Ridge stood and offered his hand, helping her up, and she brushed her hands against her jean-clad thighs.

"I'm not going to change my mind, Shiloh." She wrapped her arms around Ridge's waist, leaning in to his side. "Thank you for your help. I couldn't have done it without you."

Ridge glanced between Shiloh and her. "Did I miss something?"

"She can explain everything to you. I wanted to let you know I'm out of here. I'm heading over to the Big House, staying a few days before going back to work."

"Don't say anything to the folks, okay?" Ridge looked at Maggie, and she couldn't doubt him, not with the love shining in his eyes. "We'll be over later. I want to surprise them."

"You got it. Congratulations, you two."

They watched Shiloh grab his bag and head for the door, closing it quietly behind him.

"Where were we?" Ridge smiled at Maggie, and she knew everything was going to be okay. No, better than okay. Everything was going to be perfect.

"I think you were about to kiss me."

"Ah, Miss Maggie Mine, it will be my pleasure."

# CHAPTER TWENTY
# EPILOGUE

*W*ell, *another one bites the dust.*

Lucas watched Ridge throw his arm around Maggie's shoulders, pulling her against his side, while his momma smiled indulgently at whatever he said. Maggie laid her head on Ridge's shoulder, smiling indulgently at her fiancée. The look of pure joy on his brother's face, the happiness radiating from him, elicited a pang of envy deep inside Lucas, though he quickly quashed the emotion. He was thrilled his brother had found somebody to love. Ridge, more than most, deserved happiness, though Lucas wondered how Shiloh felt about his twin meeting his soulmate.

"Bro, good to see you. Things slowing down any?"

Lucas turned at the sound of Liam's voice. His brother had showed up a few minutes ago, late as usual. It seemed like every time he came home from Dallas for a visit, Liam was up to his eyeballs with work, always at one job site or another around Shiloh Springs. Between Dad and Liam, the Boudreau Construction Company had thrived and prospered into one of the most successful in the state. Although over the past couple of months, Dad had cut back on some of the bigger projects. Oh, not enough to consider retiring, not by a long shot. But he'd become involved in helping resolve some of the serious situations revolving around the new women his sons had fallen head over heels for. Seemed like each one came with their own personal baggage, and Dad being Dad, became their rock, the constant that held things together. Dad had taken the women—and little Jamie—under his wing like he'd done with all the boys he'd welcomed into the Boudreau clan over the years. Lucas nodded to Rafe as their brother joined them.

"The life of a reporter is never slow, bro." Lucas took a swallow of his sweet tea before adding, "I've got a couple stories I'm working on. One, in particular, is giving me fits, but I'll figure it out. Just need to do some more digging. How're you doing, Rafe? Tessa looks happy."

"She's amazing. Wedding's getting closer, and we're neck deep with planning and minute details, but Momma's helping. I swear I've never seen her so—content." Rafe grinned. "I just stand back and do the heavy lifting."

Lucas chuckled before his gaze shifted back to Ridge and Maggie. He'd met the dark-haired beauty when he'd arrived, having driven in from Dallas that afternoon, although he'd heard all about her over the last few days. Shiloh sang her praises and was working with her on setting up a nonprofit to help victims of domestic abuse, since she apparently refused to stop helping those women and children who needed her, and she was financing the new operation with her own money.

"Guys, I'm going to grab a quick shower, before Momma notices I'm still in my work clothes. I'll catch up with you in a bit." Liam clapped Lucas on the shoulder, and headed upstairs.

"I haven't seen Chance since I got here. Heard there was some excitement over by the county line. Something to do with Maggie?"

"Yeah, it's a long story. Gotta ask, did you know about Ridge working with the DEA?"

Lucas started at Rafe's question. Ridge and the DEA— nope, he'd had no idea. "No clue. When did that happen?"

"Apparently, he's been working with them for years, and none of us knew. Except Shiloh, Antonio, and Dad, though he swears he only suspected what Ridge was up to, but didn't have any cold hard facts. Turns out Ridge was working with the DEA when he met Maggie. The DEA suspected Maggie was allowing drug smugglers to run illegal contraband across her property. They tasked Ridge with finding out if she was involved, and where on her property they were moving the drugs. Of course, one look at Maggie and Ridge knew she couldn't possibly have anything to do with smuggling illegal drugs."

"I can't imagine anybody looking less like a drug runner, but looks can be deceiving."

"Oh, with Maggie still waters run deep. Maggie did a few

things that skirted the edge of the law, but that's been nipped in the bud. Chance and Shiloh are working with her, setting things up all legal and above board with her new initiative."

"Nica said something about domestic violence and a nonprofit?"

Rafe nodded. "Maggie was helping women and kids get away from their abusers, acting as a waystation or stop-gap along an underground network. The thing is, what she was doing wasn't exactly on the up-and-up, legally speaking, and skirted the edges of the law. The stress was eating her up inside. Now Momma is helping her find some property where she can set up a safe place where these women and children can get help through legal channels. Chance is arranging legal representation, getting attorneys to do pro bono work, because most of the time, they can't afford to fight their spouses or significant others in court. On the plus side, Maggie's loaded, and she's willing to invest a big chunk of money into the project."

"Underground network? The kind that helps provide new identities and relocation for the victims?" Lucas glanced across the space at Maggie, appreciating her on a whole new level. "I did some research for a story about this exact situation about six months back for a series of articles we ran. I might be able to point her toward some people who can help."

"Figured you'd know people who know people, bro." Rafe grinned and slapped him on the back before turning serious. "You sure you're okay? You look tired. Anything I can do to help?"

"I'm good, I promise. Guess I've been burning the candle at both ends for too long. I've been spending a lot of time looking for Renee. I can't shake the feeling she needs me, that she's in trouble."

Without a word, Rafe pulled him into a hug. Lucas slapped his brother on the back a couple of times, appreciating the familial show of affection and support. Rafe knew how long and hard Lucas searched for his sister, ever since they'd been separated as children and forced into the foster care system. They'd been separated almost immediately, and Renee had been adopted out, and Lucas lost all contact with his baby sister.

"I can't believe nobody's been able to find anything on her. It's not like she disappeared off the face of the earth."

"I'm not giving up. Renee's out there and I have to find her."

"You will. I know it."

"Son, good to have you home." Lucas smiled as Rafe jumped at the sound of their father's voice. He'd seen his father approaching, but Rafe's back was to him, and he hadn't heard him coming.

"It's good to be home, Dad. You're looking well."

"Can't complain. Your momma takes good care of me." Douglas turned to Rafe. "Son, mind if I have a moment with your brother?"

"Sure, Dad." Rafe put his hand on Lucas's shoulder.

"We'll talk more later, okay?"

"I'll be here."

As Rafe walked away, Lucas leaned against the doorjamb between the open foyer and the kitchen, where most of the family had gathered to celebrate Ridge and Maggie's love. He didn't fight his grin when Nica jumped onto Ridge's back and wrapped her arms around his neck, whispering something in his ear that had him laughing out loud. He loved this big, crazy family.

Douglas stood at his side, watching the mingling of his sons, his daughter, and their loved ones and smiled indulgently, before turning to Lucas and handing him a folded piece of paper. Lucas stayed silent, knowing his father would tell him what he wanted him to know when he was ready. Douglas was a stoic man, but when he loved, he loved fully and completely, and his family was the most important thing in the world.

"I had one of my Army buddies do some digging. I didn't want to say anything, not until we had something concrete."

Though he was a wordsmith and made a living finding the right words, Lucas couldn't describe the sensation that swept through him at the seriousness of his father's words, the somber inflection underlying the cautious, yet optimistic undertone. It felt like he was encased in ice, frozen, immobile except for the indrawn breath that caught in his chest.

"Tell me."

"We found Renee."

Thank you for reading Ridge, Book #4 in the Texas Boudreau Brotherhood series. I hope you enjoyed Ridge and Maggie's story.

Want to find out more about *Lucas Boudreau and the excitement and adventure he's about to plunge headfirst into?* Keep reading for an excerpt from his book, *Lucas, Book #5 in the Texas Boudreau Brotherhood. Available at all major e-book and print vendors.*

Lucas (Book #5 Texas Boudreau Brotherhood series) © Kathy Ivan

B ad weather delayed Lucas's homecoming by a couple of hours. After leaving Fort Worth, he'd had to pull over a couple of times, because the torrential rain made visibility impossible. His wipers hadn't been up to the job, even on the highest setting, and since he wasn't on a deadline, he could take his time.

The decision to head for Shiloh Springs had been a spur of the moment one, even though he'd been home a few weeks ago to celebrate with Ridge and his pretty new lady, Maggie, and catch up with the rest of the family. Rafe and Tessa's wedding was still a few months away, but he'd never seen his brother happier. Antonio and Brody also seemed to radiate happiness, especially when they were around their newfound ladies.

Exhausted from investigating his latest story, the one he'd turned in the day before, he'd crashed for twenty-four hours straight. The investigative work for the story turned ugly early on, and the more he dug, the harder it became to stay objective. He had to hand it to his brothers, because they had to deal with the scum of the earth on a regular basis. As an investigative reporter, he only came in contact with slimy characters when he was researching, making sure he had his facts straight, and that his sources were impeccable. This story, though, it got to him, crawled beneath his skin and into his brain until he saw it, lived it, breathed it even in his sleep.

Shaking his head, he realized he'd been so engrossed in his thoughts, he'd missed his exit off the interstate, and he'd have to backtrack through the southern part of Shiloh Springs county instead of heading straight to the Big House.

Heading down Main Street, everything looked the same as he had when he'd been a boy. Not a whole lot changed in the small town, and that's the way he liked it. Hc liked knowing even if he wasn't living here full time, when he came back home, everything stayed exactly as it had been when he'd left. Oh, sure, a few things changed. Shops closed. New ones opened. Folks moved away and new ones took their places. But the essence, the heart, of Shiloh Springs remained.

Silhouetted in his headlights, he spotted a woman leisurely walking along the sidewalk, and immediately his chest tightened. His breath caught in his throat, because he recognized her.

Jillian Monroe.

Jill, the woman he'd known most of his life. They'd grown up together. Gone to school together. Shared a first kiss together. She'd been his first crush, all the way back in the sixth grade. He'd hated it when she'd left and gone away to college back East. Hated every minute she was gone, though he'd never admitted it to anybody. But when she came back, she was changed. Different in a way he couldn't put his finger on. The laughing, friendly, loving Jill disappeared underneath a layer of silence, withdrawn and missing the spark she'd always had burning deep inside.

And she wouldn't talk to him. Oh, she never went out of her way to deliberately avoid him, but the spontaneity, the *joie de vivre*, her zest for life, disappeared.

Slowing down, he rolled down the passenger-side window, and called out to her. "Jill. Want a ride?"

LINKS TO BUY LUCAS:
www.kathyivan.com/books.html

# NEWSLETTER SIGN UP

Don't want to miss out on any new books, contests, and free stuff? Sign up to get my newsletter. I promise not to spam you, and only send out notifications/e-mails whenever there's a new release or contest/giveaway. Follow the link and join today!

http://eepurl.com/baqdRX

# REVIEWS ARE IMPORTANT!

People are always asking how they can help spread the word about my books. One of the best ways to do that is by word of mouth. Tell your friends about the books and recommend them. Share them on Goodreads. If you find a book or series or author you love – talk about it. Everybody loves to find out about new books and new-to-them authors, especially if somebody they know has read the book and loved it.

The next best thing is to write a review. Writing a review for a book does not have to be long or detailed. It can be as simple as saying "I loved the book."

I hope you enjoyed reading Ridge, Texas Boudreau Brotherhood.

If you liked the story, I hope you'll consider leaving a review for the book at the vendor where you purchased it and at Goodreads. Reviews are the best way to spread the word to others looking for good books. It truly helps.

# BOOKS BY KATHY IVAN

**www.kathyivan.com/books.html**

## TEXAS BOUDREAU BROTHERHOOD

Rafe

Antonio

Brody

Ridge

Lucas (Coming Soon)

## NEW ORLEANS CONNECTION SERIES

Desperate Choices

Connor's Gamble

Relentless Pursuit

Ultimate Betrayal

Keeping Secrets

Sex, Lies and Apple Pies

Deadly Justice

Wicked Obsession

Hidden Agenda

Spies Like Us

Fatal Intentions

New Orleans Connection Series Box Set: Books 1-3

New Orleans Connection Series Box Set: Books 4-7

## CAJUN CONNECTION SERIES
Saving Sarah
Saving Savannah
Saving Stephanie
Guarding Gabi

## LOVIN' LAS VEGAS SERIES
It Happened In Vegas
Crazy Vegas Love
Marriage, Vegas Style
A Virgin In Vegas
Vegas, Baby!
Yours For The Holidays
Match Made In Vegas
One Night In Vegas
Last Chance In Vegas
Lovin' Las Vegas (box set books 1-3)

## OTHER BOOKS BY KATHY IVAN
Second Chances (Destiny's Desire Book #1)
Losing Cassie (Destiny's Desire Book #2)

# ABOUT THE AUTHOR

USA TODAY Bestselling author Kathy Ivan spent most of her life with her nose between the pages of a book. It didn't matter if the book was a paranormal romance, romantic suspense, action and adventure thrillers, sweet & spicy, or a sexy novella. Kathy turned her obsession with reading into the next logical step, writing.

Her books transport you to the sultry splendor of the French Quarter in New Orleans in her award-winning romantic suspense, or to Las Vegas in her contemporary romantic comedies. Kathy's new romantic suspense series features, Texas Boudreau Brotherhood, features alpha heroes in small town Texas. Gotta love those cowboys!

Kathy tells stories people can't get enough of; reuniting old loves, betrayal of trust, finding kidnapped children, psychics and sometimes even a ghost or two. But one thing they all have in common – love and a happily ever after).

**More about Kathy and her books can be found at**

**WEBSITE: www.kathyivan.com**

**Follow Kathy on Facebook at**
**facebook.com/kathyivanauthor**

**Follow Kathy on Twitter at**
**twitter.com/@kathyivan**

**Follow Kathy at BookBub**
**bookbub.com/profile/kathy-ivan**

DISCARD

Made in the USA
Las Vegas, NV
06 March 2021

19119089R00134